Contents

Vastly Landscape

Torn asunder and turned to dust. My habitat was no more and this loss had me plummeting to whatever uncertainty awaited me in the abyss below.
i was whipped up into the air and spun around, tossed and turned. This was no wind or blizzard. It was a tornado and with the lashing deluge; a hurricane. Its force and fierceness amplified all sounds to a splitting and breaking up of my domain.
It happened so abruptly i had no chance to react and still i couldn't in my topsy-turvy bewilderment. i was unable to right myself and utilise a dragline.
i glimpsed the last wispy strands of my obliterated dwellings before it would be but a memory.
i was exposed and vulnerable and my world had become a kaleidoscope blur through the washy film of rain. Green glistening foliage followed by racing browns and a growing pallid light.
All i could think was how abruptly my circumstances had changed. Moments ago i was in clover until a violent

displacement and without my safety net, it was a cruel awakening.

Debris of varying shapes and sizes swirled lethally around me. Immense pieces missed me but smaller icy shrapnel whipped me as they bounced off of my resilient frame. It would only be a matter of time before this maelstrom ripped me apart. Or crushed me.

And then i was falling again, released from the vortex's spinning hold. Escaping the frenzy i un-expectantly landed on something feathery.

i experienced a slight lull yet the storm still persisted all around, continuing to wrench. The wind taunted me in its foreign language and threatened to dislodge me but i could not be dislodged. i clung fast to my accidental raft.

Drenched itself, this vessel also discharged welcoming warm vapours from its surface and it had a tractable material that bought me some decree of encouragement before i realised it was moving. Lumbering from side to side, i was sure whatever this behemoth was; it was completely unaware of me - its unknown passenger.

i sensed i wasn't outside any longer. There was no more wind or rain. No more of the turmoil that i had weathered. That ordeal had passed but ever danger dwells.

i began to probe my surroundings. The climate was disparate here and unlike anything i had experienced. Exposure to the elements was all i had ever known.

The air felt thicker and stale with no freshness to it. Light was different too. Intense and lacking the glow and warmth of rays i was accustomed to. Harsh on my eyes, it seemed to emit from numerous points above me.

i could make no sense of my new surroundings. It was all remote blurs and sounds were something else. Muffled echoes of exotic noises i had never heard before.

As I contemplated my next course, my abrupt change of circumstances was not over. Something shook the spot i was perched upon and a sudden repulsive piercing shrilled the air. i was expecting a voracious beast to pounce upon me when a large body swung into view and struck me a tremendous blow. Its sheer force took me off of my feet and hurtled me out into space again. My body seized with shock. My instinctive reactions were unable to react. Splashing wet particles from my damp spot joined me in a slow motion fall.

Disturbances were common, a part of my everyday where nothing was enduring. A continuing shifting existence and as often as i have trodden that ground, there was upheaval. And where was i now? Lost in a world i knew nothing about.

As i plunged into the depths of the approaching gloom, what awaited me in this vastly landscape?

As i considered my predicament i realised by contemplating upon it, i was being rational. Instinctive. i became like a speck of dust that so often snows and my descent slowed. Manipulating the gravity around me i splayed my lithe limbs outwards, a ballooning of my whole body. Buoyant on the air and following the drift down.

Peering intently into the vague distance despite the soft glow of light all around, i tried to discern what may come and readied myself for the unknown.

My surroundings were revealing themselves. Glints and colours flowed by me on both sides like shafts of rainbow blur. Incandescent eyes strobed down from above, cutting through the haze and i feared it would expose me in its glare. Big dark ominous shapes spread out around me, forming like monoliths and growing larger and mightier as i passed them. They seemed to go on forever downwards into wherever the deepness ended. These tall structures moved too, threatening in size and i agitated i would collide and be caught.

i always sought the refuge of heights. Now i was getting further and further away from that reassurance.

Falling is a common occurrence in my existence. i have learned not to fear that itself. It is where i landed that always unnerved me.

On and on i descended until the land revealed itself in its golden like topography. Stretching out as far as my constrained sight could see i regarded this luminous terrain with apprehension.

i braced myself for impact. Tensing my legs and not locking my joints, enabling a springing reaction from the shockwaves that would evenly distribute around my entire frame. i had slowed as much as my body would allow. Manipulating gravity akin to a maple seed, i could not have had a safer landing.

The gleaming surface spread out all around me in an expanse further than i could see. An unchanging plain with none of the usual wild obstacles that i was accustomed to. There was also a lack of earth and foliage in this sterile flatness. A slight breeze tickled me but it was not the wind. It felt edgy and lacked suppleness. No naturalness to it.

The leviathans pounded and pounded continually, booming back and forth randomly. Shuddering the outlandish ground all around and into my bones the vibrations trembled. Their immensity menaced over everything. Casting shadows over all like thundering clouds.

i could not linger and i cast about frantically for a shelter; a hole, corner or shadow in which i could get away from the giant's threat. The fear of being crushed propelled me.

i strained as far as my eyes would allow for something and i perceived what looked like a wide edifice with noticeable shade beneath it. i did not linger.
i scurried quickly over the smooth surface of the ground only to find myself slipping. My legs flung out beneath me and i spun in a circle.
The unexpected surface caught me by surprise. It was unlike anything i had ever traversed yet almost immediately i overcame the slippery floor with a focused hold and balance. Getting a surely grip on each of my footfalls and following through with a reflexive spring forward, i was able to gain control and confidence promptly.
i made good speed over the flat and uninterrupted terrain and used its smooth running to boldly glide until my worst fears. A shadow moved over me, spreading larger and eclipsing the golden like ground beneath me ominously.
i stopped in the hope that i wouldn't be spotted. It was futile.
i turned my head to see what it was above me and to my horror a roseate mass descended upon me. i was frozen to the spot with dread.
It unexpectedly settled onto the floor next to me. It had not crushed me. Instead it loitered at my side in a hulking, pulsating lump.
i scarpered off in the other direction and this thing moved too, just as quickly swopping over me to once again land in front of my path.
i skidded to a stop again and there it remained unmoving, reviling. Was it toying with me?
At once i scuttled off in another direction and suddenly i was plunged into darkness. Surrounded by a fleshy cocoon.

Thin shafts of light did penetrate my murky confinement, slices through the ceiling above. i could not move but i also knew the longer this continued i would feel more and more vulnerable. i had to do something and with trepidation clambered vertically over the soft clammy surface of my captor. Searching frantically for a hole. Escape.
It moved then. Upwards and upwards and light was again filling the world and i saw everything upside down. i let myself drop.
Straight away i landed on the golden floor again but before i could scramble away two large protruding parts of the grubby muscle reached down and i was deftly picked up by one of my legs.
i tried to relax as much as i could in my dangerous circumstances. i knew not to writhe and try to struggle out of this hold, it would only inflict pain. There was also the grievous possibility of a limb being pulled out of my socket.
Whether it was the clamminess of the monster's skin that allowed me to slip free i was not entirely sure but my escape was short-lived. Again.
All this ups and downs and falling was going to burst my frantically beating heart.
A shadow swooped underneath my fall, catching me and i landed in the centre of the same limb i had just slipped from. This time its centre was damper and more calloused, thicker too. A pulse throbbed from inside it beneath my feet. It felt a little similar to rocking of a large leaf but there was nothing familiar or reassuring about it. It had an organic odour of rank perspiration.
Abruptly this slab rapidly rose into the air and its force flattened me in its folds until i was confronted with the

most frightening and disgusting thing i had ever laid my eyes upon.

Enveloping my entire world loomed a globe with dark thick tangled growth atop and its skin was anaemic. Two small circular reflective balls moved erratically from side to side and between them a protruding thing twitched up and down. Beneath a further much larger aperture gaped open to reveal an obscurity of nauseating stench.

For a brief moment i caught a glimpse of myself in the two mirrored balls and i recoiled with alarm at the comprehension of my size. The futility and vulnerability of how small i was.

Though i had overcome that reality a long time ago, seeing my miniscule self, reflected back in those probing, dissecting optics horrified me.

My frightened jolt pitched me off the sweaty limb and once again i fell. No aerofoil descent this time, i let myself freefall and prepared myself for a much tougher landing in my eagerness to get away.

It seemed it was all i was doing since my upheaval and surely after all the attempts i could finally elude my pursuer. i even forego the use of my integral lifeline. i wanted no more attachment with this grotesque giant anymore then i wanted to look into those terrorising eyes.

As soon as i hit the ground without injury, i was sprinting towards shadows. i had never been so fast and agile.

Crawling and concealing myself in its dark recesses, this structure gave me a degree of shelter and safety for now.

Had i eluded the monster? Had it lost me here in the dusty darkness of my hidey-hole and given up the tormenting pursuit? Ever the danger dwells.

i climb, climb, climb its vertical side and with its overhead, this secrete corner offered me a niche where i could remain watchful and regain composure after my exhausting and panic-stricken ordeal.

The little light that reached this far into the shelter bounced from the floor and occasionally a flicker of a shadow moved by outside. The leviathans pounded and pounded sending thumping vibrations up the structure's frame. Frequently the whole construction would shift under an immense weight above, creaking and groaning in its joints and then the giant and its shadow would depart and i heard the structure's relief.

This place i had discovered by accident, brought in on the back of a lumbering leviathan and launched into a world i never knew existed.

i did not believe i could find my way back out into the elements.

How long before darkness descended? It would bring a degree of cover and then i could crawl about this mid-world only knowing things through touch. Its newness and unfamiliarity felt relatively tame. In all its peculiar perils, this was a place i would adapt to with nimbleness. i have done before and i will again.

i heard the faintest of notes. So indistinct that i initially ignored it as some framework but when it twanged again i discovered its source and only because my nocturnal sight caught its sly movements.

Above and further along and emerging from the blackest shadows i spotted its eyes scintillating like water. It's reach and strides unmistakable. Elongated limbs revealing its bigness; three times the girth of me and menacing for it. Its tusks almost the size of my head glistened and i began to sweat with fear. i could smell its hunger and imagine it cleaning and polishing its fangs with its salivating.

Terrifyingly it was the only familiar thing in this unfamiliar world.

i would not win this fight. It would overcome me with its size and strength. i had come across its kind before. My unforgiving brethren.

i did what i only could and let myself drop the short distance and made my escape.

i hastily emerged from under my brief shelter and ventured precariously into the lights again. Laid bare and fearful of the leviathans, i suddenly noticed the pounding and bustling of earlier had ceased.

Scrambling forward and away from the structure, i glanced back and observed i was not being pursued by my nemesis neighbour. Had it chosen to remain in its dark territory and it too, afraid to come out into the open because its larger size was fair game?

i did not stop. i continued running because i myself was now exposed and i needed cover or height.

i approached an upright that stretched out either side of me. On and on it disappeared into a cloudy light above. This i concluded would give me the alleviation i needed. Away and above the leviathans.

Then i felt a slight change. A difference in the air and the hairs on my body tinkled. It felt a little similar to the external elements and gradually escalating the closer i approached. Curiously i had a need to know what to expect of this other world. Prepare myself for any potential dangers if this was to be my new environment.

A growing frigid blast pushed against me. Got under my skin and into my joints. Goosebumps followed. So vigorous and located it was developing, it hampered my progress slightly. It was like the wind but not. Harsher, more condensed. With a little more effort i pushed myself.

The source grew into view. An elongated rectangular aperture covered with a menacing mesh at the foot of the wall. It had the appearance of a cage and the mouth akin to a giant mechanical creature. Inside it, strands of dust danced in the gust like dribbling tendrils.

My eyes were now stinging from the habitual blasting yet i caught a glimpse into its deep pitch of blackness. Its chillness unnerved all the fibres in my body.

Where did it lead to i speculated only briefly. Here my inquisitiveness ended. i would never venture into its wintery stark depths. It would be needless and i would learn to avoid these rattling fissures by the sound of its belly.

i turned away from the whispering hole and headed for the upright. Up is what i sought.

Initially the rampart had a smoother, urbane surface and again if i did not accentuate my grip, i would slip.

Climb, climb, climb.

Very soon the surface changed texture. Course, thickly soft and easy underfoot of all the other surfaces i had experienced so far in this contrasting environment.

By now i had encountered many different unknowns and had prepared myself for the strange and precarious. This world had made me cautious again after complacency and soon its strangeness would become second nature to my instincts. Taste and touch stimulate my navigation. i would adapt again.

The vertical rose and rose continuously as i scaled its face with confident ease. Climb, climb, climb, leaving the ground below me to shrink away and disappear into the hazy distance.

Clumps of fuzz clung to this easily navigated terrain and it smelt dust imbued. The higher i scaled, the warmer it became and it had nothing to do with exertion. Brighter too with a potency unlike the sun. Above me an intensifying artificial glare emitted light and heat the more i continued and i was sure i would eventually become too close and scorched. Blinding and searing, the beams congregated like stars and i would learn to avoid them too like so many of the dangers of this new world. The ceiling of daylight sky.

An immense object loomed into view where it protruded from the wall. Its edges sparkled bluntly and it surface was a myriad of contours and bumps with many cavities.

i put a apprehensive foot upon it, probing it. It felt pulpy, wood like. Crawling cautiously i clambered over the irregular terrain and scrutinised the many dingy crevices scattered about where from inside ancient dust tickled my sense of smell. Pockets dense with garden grey gossamer but here it lacked consistency and silkiness. Dry and brittle. Once again this familiarity gave me hope that my kind could survive and inhabit here. With its possible hidey-holes, it was a spot to consider for later.

The absence of water was salient here. So far, arid. It was not an immediate concern. i could survive on very little for spun out and i was certain too that i would discover moisture. It prevailed in even the harshest and strangest of environments. With perseverance, sustenance too can habitually be found.

Peering along its length, the shimmering bumpy surface appeared only a border to another far larger tract. Levelled with random ripples, smudges and occasional thicker blobs of varying hues. Its ground was a mixture of light and dark shapes. The more i ventured further into its centre the colours revealed patterns, images. A vivid expanse.

Long before, i emerged into life as i know it. Without defence or guidance i crawled. Learning the rigorous passages of what was necessity. Innate mechanisms grew and guided me and these instincts furthered me to endure. And still i do in all the diversity. Since the upheaval of my previous dwellings, i have been introduced to a world so different from the elements i had been accustomed to.

Yet nature is no different here. Lifelines will be destroyed and lifelines will be rebuilt. The danger ever dwells.

Eventually i reached the golden like edge again. It seemed this surrounded this varied plain. Clambering over it again and avoiding all of the small rifts i left the rolling plateau and spotted something further on.

Its conspicuous whiteness caught my eyes, shimmering like a puddle. Approaching, it appeared as a raised platform or insert that was clearly much smaller then the one i had just discovered. About the size of a large leaf, it was bright white and reflective.

Again with trepidation, i placed a leg upon it and found it greasy. There was also something clean and smooth to its make-up. As i almost glided over its skin, i noticed minute markings beneath it transparent surface. In black symmetrical etchings displayed in horizontal lines unfamiliar and occurring frequently. Some of these symbols were larger than others and bolder in places. Foreign to me of course but intrigued i was by their meaning, purpose.

It would never understand them.

It was something of this milieu that it had inadvertently been thrown into.

A place where it had no right to be but nevertheless a sanctuary perhaps and a preferable chance on survival.

It could take some comfort from that because of the object it was perched upon and if it could read behind its calculating, scrutinising eight eyes; it would reveal something of its new world …….

Joseph Wright of Derby
(1734–1797)

**An Experiment on a Bird in the
Air Pump,** 1768

A lecturer demonstrates the creation of a vacuum to a family. A white cockatoo (an exotic bird, unlikely in fact to have been used for this experiment) is imprisoned in a glass flask from which the air is being extracted by a pump. The candlelit setting is characteristic of Wright's interest in dramatic contrasts of light and shade.

Oil on canvas

NG725. Presented by Edward Tyrrell, 1863

1143 ·))

Afterword

I am always attracted in the challenge of writing from an unorthodox perspective. I also wanted to attempt writing something in 'real-time' too.

March 2016

Room 56

The silence was golden and the shadows smouldered.
So quiet you could almost hear the excited yells of dust as they free-falled.
In the darkness it could have been a Mausoleum.
In a way that was what the room contained; paintings of allegedly genuine people from hundreds of years ago but were now dead.
Supposedly.
What little light there was seemed to emanate from the grey walls as if it was coated with radioactive paint and the puddle like polished wooden flooring gave the space a superficial reflective illumination.
Then, the softest and simplest of musical notes was heard; an elegant sound with a faithful balance of melodiousness and audibleness, enough to ring around the room courtesy.
Ever so subtly more keys were introduced, harmoniously.
It was akin to the good vibrations of angels.
Hard to believe yet authentically that was what it was. A graceful melody with a catchy and enchanting heart soaring

chorus, the most uplifting sonnet your ears would ever hark to. Lifted your spirit and made you rejoice in its blessedness. You believed there was a heaven and that the Lord himself was…..

"OH FOR GOD'S SAKE! GIVE IT A REST WILL YA?"

The music stopped as abruptly as the beheading of a tenor tenor-ing.

A uniformed gasp as deep as a chasm echoed in the room.

Then from that painting of an apse with two Angels playing an odd guitar and a miniature harp, a diminutive voice squeaked sheepishly, "We need to practise."

"Well you've been practising for forever and its still shite."

Another choral gasp followed, this time as deep as the Mariana Trench and because that was underwater no sound was heard. It was a synchronized silently mouthed 'O' by all instead.

They couldn't believe it. It was blasphemous.

"You.., spoke….. Brother." one of them said tentatively on tenterhooks.

"Damn, damn, DAMN…..! I know, I KNOW!" Annoyed with himself, he screamed "Arrrrrrrrgghhhhh!"

Their eyes flitted to one another disconcertingly.

"Arrrrgh! Errrrr! Arggggh! Rrrraaaaahh!" he continued, testing his unaccustomed vocal chords that had not been used in literally ages. The hand that held a rolled up scroll shook it up and down like a baby's rattle.

Everyone around remained meek. Keeping a respectful and frightful distance as it was all terribly frightful and disrespectful.

He was a podgy Franciscan monk with a small round head of Lilliputian features. Two crimped worry lines skid-marked across his forehead and his sideburns had observably AWOL-ed. His hair was the same colour as the hefty brown sack of a robe he wore.

Shaking his head like Punch to Judy he lamented, "Nearly six hundred years ...." That was how old his painting was; as were all the others too. "......I remained moral and chaste..." Most Brothers and Monks didn't choose a vow of silence but he did. Maybe he was bored!

"......Evince my resolution to my God, but there is only so much I could put up with, then THAT BLOODY....." he applied his metaphorical and metaphysical brakes.

"Forgive me Lord. Als ich kan (In Dutch it meant 'as well as I can'). It's that repetitive infernal racket. On and on and on, every day the same irritating tune....." the brakes were off again and he was accelerating faster and louder, ".....YOU NEVER PLAY ANYTHING ELSE. Never try to. Probably couldn't. Wouldn't want to hear it anyway. BURN YOUR BLASTED INSTRUMENTS!"

Then his ire abruptly dissolved and he shamefully checked himself.

"Sorry. I will go to confession for those impure thoughts....." he started again, ".......... But I still want to SHOVE YOUR INTRUMENTS RIGHT UP BOTH OF YOUR ANGELIC RECTUMS!" He blurted schizophrenically.

His company remained as aghast as the Holy Ghost suddenly finding itself unemployed.

"SEE! Look what you have done to me. Not only broken my devout silence but now have planted the devil seed in my unadulterated musings. Never once did I think such debasing thoughts. What have you done to me? FUCK! SHIT! BUGGER! ARSE.....! He was still swinging the scroll in his hand around like an over-zealous policeman with a truncheon.

"….. Cock! Fuck! Aaaaaarrrrghh!" He began to sob then with the guilt, his beetroot face streaming with tears.

Nothing was said by anyone. They didn't dare to.

The angels held their un-playing instruments like stale celery. Others just stared into their books or manuscripts like it was the new edition of 'Heat' and some gazed down at the floor like it was a recent art installation.

All were awkwardly shuffling as if they had been invited to a bar mitzvah and the meat that the Jehovah's Witnesses catering staff had provided was pork.

Then the Franciscan monk blew his nose like a trumpet and announced chokingly that he would again start a vow of silence and apologised for his unbecoming behaviour.

Everyone vocally stampeded at once, pleased for him.

"Well done chap."

"Best thing you can do."

"Hoorah!"

"Do what you do best Brother."

"Good luck."

"Go Bro go!"

He nodded his abashed head while wiping his eyes at the round of applause and encouragement.

It wasn't long before he resumed his habit of un-rolling and re-rolling the scroll in his hand in pointless pedantic silence like he had always done. The last six hundred years.

When all the others saw this, they felt all was well again while muttering "Thank God!" under their breath.

Their content sighs rustled the barriers sanguinely.

The angels with their instruments dared not start playing again. Yet.

All was hushed.

Then there was a faint peep, like a squeezing through a narrow crack. Barely got wind of and promptly, prudently ignored by all. Many eyes gave furtive glances but nothing was said and the silence resumed politely.

Until…..

"Err…. Excuse me. Has anyone lost a ring?" asked a feeble voice.

It belonged to a young man with a sour puss of a face and a nose that looked like it had been dipped in paint stripper.

There was a resounding groan all around akin to a group of restless Rabbis' without pupils.

"No" someone replied prickly.

He only wanted to return it to its rightful owner. Someone somewhere had lost it.

The same way he had lost the plot. The lights were on but there was no one in at the inn.

On the other side of the room another portrait of a man named Léal Souvenir could not decide who he wanted to watch as his head ping-ponged back and forth.

He had a monkey-ish face and was wearing what resembled a grimy tea towel on his head and was garishly garbed in what resembled a red bath towel.

One of the paintings of the two that had his attention was The Magdalen Reading; a woman sitting on the floor on a tangerine pillow engrossed in a book. She wore an abundantly lush green dress and a Mona Lisa smile was perpetually pleased on her face.

An alabaster jar of ointment was on the floor next to her and some of the rooms occupant's imagination often got the better of them and would wonder what was really in that jar. Not the ointment or perfume that was meant to be inside but this week the consensus was that it contained Jesus's Balls!

She looked up occasionally but noticed no one. She was very intent on finishing her Jackie Collins novel.

The other person that was figuratively and unbeknownst to him hitting the tennis ball back was of a man reading a letter; Léal's rival of sorts but it was only an invention of Léal's envious mind. On the opposite side of the room in a warped wood wormed frame Saint Ivo had a chipped bowl shaped haircut and his chocolate brown eyes intently perused a letter. Occasionally he would murmur something incomprehensibly unimportant as he read it.

Whenever Léal Souvenir peered over at the Magdalen a cocky expression appeared on his face while he swaggeringly straightened his tea towel again and again. He was constantly vying for her merciful magnetism. Yet when he checks out the other side of the court – St. Ivo, his brow deepens like two bruised and miserable clouds, his green eyes turning as bitter and sour as two jealous olives praying to be picked first.

"Oi! Ivo. How many more times you gonna read that?" He yelled yob-like while glancing over to the Magdalen to see if she had heard his bravado that was plain Alpha Male-ism!

Still she remained tranquilly engrossed in her book and Ivo was a fully paid up and haloed member of the ignoramuses.

"Surprised that letter hasn't turned to dust by now Ivo?"

He was being ignored twofold but still he ploughed on like a runaway tractor.

"You reading porn there, Ivo the Horny?"

Ivo would not be plagued but it did not stop Léal from his continual attempts at provocation even if it was akin to poking a brick wall with a pansy.

"You wrote it yourself, I bet! Making out your popular or something! Got an imaginary pen pal there? Or is it a summons for not paying your Beano subscription?"

Meanwhile the young man with the ring now addressed the newlywed Arnolfini's.
"Good day to you both. Congratulations are in order." he curtsied uncouthly. "You didn't happen to lose a ring did you?"
"Give it a rest Gollum." Someone said.
And another someone sniggered.
"No-ooo! Of course we haven't." The newlyweds replied spunkily, simpering at each other like Barbie and Ken.
A dirty cotton-ball scruff of a dog ran pointless attention seeking circles around the couple. It seemed to be yapping but no sound was heard.
Proudly showing off their lucky dip rings, Mrs Arnolfini heralded "Look! We are wearing ours." She giggled like an aroused gibbon.
She was dressed in what plainly looked like a balloon of a maternity dress. As large and long as it gathered on the floor, it could have fitted a tree. The sleeve holes so huge you could fall into them and not touch the sides.
"Still living in sin though," interrupted that wife from the portrait titled 'The Man and a Woman.'
Mrs. Arnolfini's grin plunked and was lost in the folds of her dress. "Pardon me?" She said.
It was all the encouragement that wife needed. "You're up the duff and only just married. Shameful!"
She appeared squeaky clean sinless but that was far from her real pouting pious personality. She had a sardonic face and when she spoke sounded like she had a peg on her nose. Her head and shoulders were covered in a vast white

shawl which made people think that she needed 'Head & Shoulders.'

Her husband had a red turban lounging on his head. He was trying to look Lawrence-y of Arabia but looked more like 'Moe' from the 'Three Stooges.'

Looking upon everything happening around them with an air of snobbery and as old school as the Scriptures they believed themselves to be better than most. To them everyone else was a heretic!

The young man with the ring was forgotten as per the course. In as much a way as he could within a frame, he shuffled off.

"My wife is not pregnant." Mr. Arnolfini looked like death warmed up and wore a hat the size of a temple and attire that made the Grim Reaper gravely reconsider his wardrobe. The rest of his facial features were dwarfed by the largest nose in the world, shaped like the bow of a ship. It meant his nose always arrived before he did.

"Wasn't talking to you, Noah's Ark nose."

He became as speechless as a sinkhole and the boneless dog barked silently and loyally like it had something to say on the matter too.

"Slut!" that wife spat.

"How dare you call our dog a slut?"

"I didn't. I was calling you a slut, SLUT!" She emphasised the last 'Slut' like it was something akin to excrement. "But because you have brought your whelp into this, all it is, is a stinking stool-dropping hairy bag of flea infected testis! Wouldn't even wipe my shoes on him."

Someone tutted.

The dog confused with the attention and the insult, whimpered silently off under Mrs. Arnolfini's dress; its tail literally tucked between its legs and feathering its balls and you could off thrown a coin into Mrs. Arnolfini's gawking mouth and made a wish.

She turned to her husband for furtherance but he was acting a convincing bystander until he was figuratively kick-started by his wife's 'say something' stare.

"Now look here woman…." He started, rubbing his figurative shin. "…. That's no way to…" He could not finish.

"I told you to stay out of this Titanic nose."

He was silenced this time like a sacrificial lamb.

"Probably only married because you were forced to by your stigmatized parents. Oh, what they must be going through. The embarrassment! Thus, twas deemed the virtuous thing to do in the eyes of the Lord. A marriage of convenience. And we all know what the church thinks of women like you?"

"What do you mean?"

"You had a bun in the oven sinner while you walked the aisle."

"For the umpteenth time, I AM NOT PREGNANT!" She had raised her quivering and quacking voice.

"No need to shout, TART!" That wife shouted. "The neighbours might hear and we couldn't have that could we. What would they say? And what would your parents think?"

"For the gossip becomes Gospel." Someone quipped in.

Mr Arnolfini cowardly whispered in her ear, "Send her to Coventry dear."

"Yes, you are right. Let's pray. Pray for patience and pray for her."

They started the mantra, "Als ich kan." Again and again they repeated it while spurning that wife who was now sticking her nose so far up, it was ready for ascension.

There was an animated ruffling sound in the background. Many eyes gave furtive glances but nothing was said.

As the Arnolfinis' continued chanting, "Our Creator, Our most Holy, Our God……." they were interrupted.

Someone else wanted to have a go.

"He's not my creator. I believe in the Almighty." Interjected Léal. "I mean how serious can you take someone who has a pile of laundry on his head?" He was pointing exaggeratedly at the portrait of Jan van Eyck.

To the majority of them in this room, van Eyck was their deity. Well they believed he created them and bore the psalm that formed their worship. Their dogmatic dogma!

"Atheist!" that wife hissed back serpent-like.

"How can I be an atheist when I believe in a God, THE God, my God and not you're made up one for God's sake?"

"Shut up Baboon-face."

He guffawed, "You ain't no oil painting yourself."

Someone sniggered.

She didn't know what to say to that. So chagrined for a change, she failingly disguised it as a snobbish snub.

"As well as I can, as well as I can….." Léal continued addressing the Arnolfinis.' "Yeah, you keep saying that, as well as I can hear ya, as well as I can hear ya and you know what? I've heard enough…" He paused dramatically, arms raised to the celestial skies,

"I see it. A vision from above….. As well as I can kill, as well as I can kill…." He repeated it louder and louder and more mockingly, intently unhinged each time. "AS WELL AS I CAN KILL, AS WELL AS I CAN KILL…." He looked like someone who was ready to bring about Armageddon. "You scared now?" he finished dramatically menacing.

He had put the fear of God into them as well as the notion he was of the mentally unstable and liable to break the Sixth Commandment.

"Will you ALL stop fucking arguing!" It was a biblical crack of thunder: Akin to the voice of God. But it was the usually but not lately, silent Franciscan. Losing his rag again!

"Have you never got anything nice to say to each other?" He shrugged his shoulders like a long suffering and overloaded donkey. "Why can't you all get along? Love thy neighbour and…"

"Oh, here he goes. Preaching now. It had to come." intervened Léal.

"AAAARGH! You are all so…... SO ARSE!" He was beating his chest with the scroll, not in pointless penitence but in utter frustration.

"On and on and on with your constant bickering and bitching. Griping like geriatric juveniles and dragging each other down like cynical quicksand. Christians like you SHOULD be thrown to the lions."

He was on a roll now. Yeah, right! Like a rolling boulder coming down on the man that gave up pushing it up the hill.

"Ooohh..! The language." Léal proclaimed. "Not so devoted now eh Brother? Once you start you can't stop."

"Fer……, fer……, fer… Oh bollocks!" He stuttered. "Leave me alone."

But Léal didn't. "Making up for lost time now bro. The earlier outbursts were not enough eh? Got the gift of the gab again and you're not giving it up this time. Been missing it for oh so long, so sod the vow of silence! Many opportunities from the past when you very much wanted to say something. Join in and voice all your opinions. All that built up anger was boiling away inside you like the pits of Hades. What you've always wanted to proclaim would put the Spanish Inquisition in the shade."

The Franciscans' body language lamented and he humbly said, "Oh God! That's how I feel. For the life of me I could not say anything. For so long the burning itch, my very own cross to bear. I yearned to and yet knew it would be wrong. Remained on the moral side of right but I could not help myself."

He had everyone's attention now like that bloke doing his Sermon on the Mount but with a mike.

"I'm afraid of what comes out of my mouth, my foul blue mouth. All the things I want to say and every single word lay wastes to my vow of silence. It's disrespectful to you and my promise to Our Lord." He sighed the sigh of Doves that had only ever seen cats and dogs fight.

"It does not matter anyway. It only comes out like some form of premature verbal ejaculation. I'm sorry."

The respectful silence that followed after his speech was divine. They all emphasized, understood that like any man, the temptation was....

"SAY! What if someone steps on your little toe when you're on a vow of silence? Can you yell out and call them a bloody oaf?"

It was Léal. "… Or you see a fire? Can you warn anybody? Shout for help? Only asking like."

The Franciscan was not falling asleep for that Trojan horse. He had again become as tolerant and patience as all the angels in Heaven. While Léal imagined himself on stage at the Comedy Store: The John the Baptist of blasphemy.

"Okay, how about if someone accuses you off stealing more than your allowance of toilet paper in the monastery.

You didn't do it but you are still going to be punished by the whip? Can you protest your innocence then? Can you yell out in pain as the lashings lacerate your body? Hmmm....? Do you talk to yourself? I bet you do? Forget yourself for a moment and speak aloud a thought. We all do it. There's no denying it. You know what? I think you're all charlatans. Crooked as a counterfeit! It's a common misconception that Brothers and Monks don't speak. It's balderdash!"

As far as everyone else listening in was concerned, this was the best recreation since sliced Communion bread.

Totally offhandedly and unconnected Léal continued, "Let's talk about chastity eh? You guys ain't meditating. No, not all the time and…. TIME you have a lot of on your wanking hands. You must be masturbating constantly because it's what…. we…. guys… have…. TO DO. It's not biologically healthy to keep all that lust and love juice bunged up there. Its lover's balls for you celibates, plain and simple and it has to come out eventually. It's natural, baby. Bet you're bashing the bishop all the time?"

"Fuck off!" the Franciscan uttered. His imaginary angel wings vanished off the face of the earth in a puff of pluming feathers.

Then there was a timid discharge that sounded like a muffled trumpet. These rippling reverberations were still ignored.

"Sorry. Umm…, has anyone lost a ring?" He was waving it about now like a winning raffle ticket. He so much wanted to return it to its owner that he believed must be so distraught.

But really he was bringing attention to the fact that he nothing better to do with himself.

"Will you stop bleating on about that bloody ring?" Léal blared.

"Ah, leave him alone." Said the 'portrait of a young man' who never said much.

"You're only saying that because you feel sorry for him. Because he has a conk that looks like ravioli."

Someone sniggered.

With his little baby boy face and his homemade wig, the 'portrait of a young man' felt as worthwhile as a split condom.

"Join the club of lemons with your mate 'Penis-ring' there." Léal added.

Tucked away in one eclipsed corner of the room is yet another painting of the Virgin and Child. So teensy-weensy that the other paintings had given up yonks ago trying to hear what she had to say. She was just too piddling small. It was like watching and waiting for an unripe sketch of an apple. Fruitless!

Yet it was the other representation of the same subject to the left of this painting that was heard.

The shrieking child.

"Could you keep the noise down?" It was not asked.

It was that wife again and she was addressing The Virgin and Child before a fire screen.

The 'portrait of a young man' who never said much said "You could say please?"

"I was not talking to you!" That wife scolded.

The 'portrait of the young man' who never said much resumed not saying anything. He remained as wordless as Judas at the Last Supper.

That wife's attention U-turned back to the mother and wailing child. "Put a cork in him!"

The Virgin had spun out permed hair like sun bleached Ivy falling from her long-faced face. Spider like fingers held her breast and baby; the Christ child who was wrinkled and grey resembled a resurrected corpse. He already looked a thousand years old!

The Virgin petitioned "Please understand." While raising one hand that gestured at her child sympathetically.

"We were understanding! We understood. Now after ages of that racket, we do not want to understand anymore." It was not an understatement.

"My child is not well." She was wobbling her left rigid breast to emphasise this. "Always hungry."

The husband took his snail's pace time to look away for disgusted appearances but found it titillating. He said "Her breasts are….."

"…. Out and exposed for all to see." miffed that wife. "Put 'em away. You do that in private."

"I am in my privates." The Virgin replied not guilty.

The husband tried to clear his flabbergasted airways. It was all getting too much for him this innuendo.

"You're not even a virgin." The wife followed scornfully.

"Yes I am."

"Poppycock, with some other man's cock. That's what it is. You were putting it about."

"No I wasn't. It was an Immaculate Conception."

"Virgin my anus! You're a liar."

"No I am not. God told me."

"Call the fruit-cake squad! You're certifiably mad. Not even fit to be a mother. Call social services too while you're at it."

The Child shrilled the shrill of a thousand devil spawn and the Virgin cooed and rocked the Child while trilling, "There, there, there, my baby Jesus. It's alllllllll-right!"

"It's a monster. A wailing demon. No human child should bawl that much." That wife was laying it on with a trowel now.

"Please don't say that about my child. He just needs more food. A normal, healthy appetite my Jesus has."

"He never stops. He'll eat all of us one day."

"He will be King one day." She said as she kissed his forehead motherly and gushingly proud while he groped and squeezed his mother's empty and slumping sac of a breast.

"And I will be a hippopotamus." That wife guffawed.

"Are you not?" Léal interjected.

Someone sniggered.

In the background was heard an uncouth honk. Life went on.

Ignoring that comment and the fart, that wife resumed, "You're a prostitute. No better than that whore over there." She pointed at the Magdalen.

"Oh no she isn't!" Léal was sticking up for her even though she did not notice his gallantry. Not even the Four Horsemen of the Apocalypse was going to drag her away from her Jackie Collins novel now. She was near the end.

"She's reformed, hence her name. The Magdalen. It means reformed prostitute."

"Pah! Once a slag always a slag." That wife expounded.

Everyone was riveted as hammered rivets. It was the latest twitter that everyone wanted to be involved in. But the Magdalen, she did not look up.

"You're a whore." That wife harangued the Virgin. "Even your husband Joseph is beginning to believe the gossip. He can't understand all this Immaculate Conception malarkey. Poor chap is now doubting his faith when you told him you were pregnant with the Son of God. Preposterous! That the

Lord put his wife up the duff! Ain't exactly the next door neighbour is he or some bloke down the local? I mean it's not like he can punch God's lights out is it? I don't blame him for thinking some other fella was poking you and damn well wanting to know who this Tom, Dick or Adam is so he can go around and knock his bloody block off. My wife's been rogered by a spirit. Bollocks! What a crock of ghost shit!"

The sniggerer sniggered.

"It's enough to drive Joseph into leprosy. I sympathise for him. You don't deserve the carpenter. He'd probably want to crucify the man that got you pregnant but you can't put God on crucifix can you? God forbid! You're a liar, a HARLOT and should be stoned." That wife finished unforgivably.

The silence that followed was similar to when three wise men arrived after travelling for many, many miles with anticipated gifts that were simply crap presents. Best not say anything, Mary and Joseph had agreed!

For the owner of the ring to turn up was like waiting for the Second Coming.

No one was forthcoming. Not at all interested.

So he continued examining the gold ring he was holding in his hand like an impoverished pawnbroker.

"Oi! Ring boy!"

He looked around hopefully and eagerly to whomever was addressing him, maybe now he could return the ring he so much wanted to. This is it! At last be finally ennobled for his neighbourly efforts. That what he thought. More like nobbled!

It was Léal that was calling him of course, "…. See that inscription on the wall behind you?"

He nodded bright-eyed and bushy tailed, knew it only too
well. It was his guiding light, a motto of sorts that he
fetched all the way.
"It quotes 'Lord let this cloud pass over.' Doesn't it?"
"Yes." He replied ecstatically.
"Well I think it should say 'Lord let this clot -YOU- pass
away!'"
His ear to ear grin dwindled, dropped and disappeared
between the floorboards.
The sniggerer was heard doing what he always did.
Feeling pretty smug with himself Léal glanced over to the
Magdalen.
Nothing. She hadn't even noticed him.
Of course she hadn't.
But he did see Ivo ogling her.
Of course he was.
"Hey Ivo! What the fuck is it you're reading there? C'mon
man, tell us." Léal still persisted.
Curiosity was going to run over this cat. Reverse and do it
once again.
He decided to tell, let them all know. It was said to be good
to share your problems. It lifted the weight of the world off
your shoulders, halved the burden and made things better.
Soon he would discover it was all tarradiddle!
He took a deep brave breath, "….. I've been diagnosed
with 'Pruritu Ani.'" He divulged emphatically and
embarrassedly.
"Eh?" they chorused.
"Itchy bum."
There was an apparently sympathetic silence.
Many eyes pin-balled off each other.
Then they all burst out laughing.
All of them. Every single one.

The painting of an Apse with two Angels and their instruments chortled symphonically. Ring Boy tittered and the Portrait of the Young Man who never said much snorted.

The Arnolfinis' screeched like monkeys and their dog, pausing from licking his balls popped his head out from under his Mrs's dress to cock his head sideways, curious to the commotion.

That Wife and her Husband even broke their habit of eternal judgement to howl like rapturous hyenas.

The Virgin in the 'Virgin and Child before a fire-screen' painting could be seen laughing but because it was teensy-weensy couldn't be heard and the other 'Virgin and Child in an interior, well that virgin was crackin' up, her jaw hurting and her shrieking Child even stopped wailing to wonder what everyone else was doing and joined in with happy dribbling gurgles.

The Franciscan who had once again broken his vow even though he promised himself that it would be the last time and would never do it again was apologising laughingly, managing to say that he could not help it for all the glory of the Promised Land.

The usually preoccupied Magdalen even stopped reading the last few pages of her Jackie Collins novel to giggle like a teenager.

Léal was beside himself in stitches, splitting his sides. Creasing up!

And the person who was always sniggering did not snigger no more. He, Edward Grimston, far from grim, bellowed like ringing bells.

Equally the revered and un-stirring portrait of Van Eyck came alive to gregariously guffaw like a dotty deity.

And while the laughter echoed resoundingly around Room 56 and everybody was enjoying themselves at his expense, Ivo felt like hanging himself with his Rosary beads.

And let's not forget in another reserved corner of the room there was a Portrait of a Lady.

She had on her head what looked like a giant's collectible thimble covered in a giant's pocket sized tissue. Looking as aloof as an Egyptian effigy, she was trying to control her emotions. So well did she restrain that the tears of laughter pouring from her eyes threaten to run, soak and spoil the paint and herself. So hard did she concentrate on not bursting out with belly laughs that the pressure was released somewhere else.

An eruption of a bottom burp!

The room's laughter abruptly ceased.

All eyes magnetised to the instigator, the one they knew who had been breaking wind records all that time. They had never brought attention to that occurrence and had never embarrassed her by mentioning it but now, well they all burst out laughing again.

Even more convulsed, louder and more tickled then last time.

She began to let go and really chortle now and she was not clenching her bum cheeks anymore either. The inborn reflexes came bountifully.

Soon dawn came. In its own time and drowsingly stretching itself awake it pulled itself from out under the covers of night. Its morning rays of light yawning through.

Akin to a slow suspenseful fade to black but in reverse the room brightened; the light percolating like a very weak and very milky coffee.

It was time for them to revert. Become static and soundless again, lifeless portraits and cease giving themselves a hard time.

"Sshh!" one of them warned as the echoing footsteps of staff could be heard starting to arrive in preparation for the gallery opening.

But one of them could not resist a final shot over the bow.

"Hussy!"

Afterword

When I started this story there was one painting in Room 56 that is not there now? 'The Virgin and Child in an Apse with Two Angels.' It's a shame it isn't there now; makes this story feel a little less complete if you were reading it while in that room, which I recommend. But when will the Art Handling department finally return it? Who fucking knows?

October 2012

THE JOB

She entered the rear of the gallery on Orange Street.
Windswept blonde hair matched her carefree strides. She wore an open turquoise North Face jacket over a baggy grey jumper and loose black slacks on her slender six foot physique. On her feet were bright blue Skechers and she carried a large Cass Art plastic bag over her shoulder.
In the lobby she approached the Information desk with a smile but the two guards sitting behind it were engrossed in a conversation and failed to notice.
She picked up a gallery guide, perused it and made up her mind to purchase one. She deposited a £1 coin into the collection box.
The male and female guards had barely acknowledged her; only the young man gave her a cursory glance as he continued to talk enthusiastically about an Indiana Jones movie.
With guide in hand, she strode off leisurely towards the ladies toilets situated to the left of the lobby. A staircase led up to the main floor of the gallery and as she passed it,

she took a glance to her right where another set of steps led down to Gallery A and there she noticed the doors were open.

Satisfied she entered the toilets and saw a large lady rearranging the straps of her substantial bra under her squeezed blouse. No one else was present in the toilets as she walked by checking each vacant cubicle and stepped into the end one, locking it behind her.

She placed the toilet lid down, sat on it and waited.

Shortly she heard the large lady leave. She then proceeded to tear up the gallery guide in her hand into many small pieces, letting them fall into a pile at her feet. With that done she then pulled out of the dispenser, sheets of toilet paper and began to tear them into small pieces too, adding them to the pile.

While doing that she heard the ladies' door open and two more women entered together chatting about flowers and a woman called Caroline. Locking themselves into neighbouring cubicles they continued their conversation like they were having afternoon tea in Claridges.

She had stopped her tearing.

After what seem like an age having to listen to their inane chatter, she heard the toilets flushing, the rustling of clothing, the scuffle of high heels, and the release of door locks followed by the running of water and the blasting of dryers. Before long the toilets ceased activity and all was quiet again.

She resumed her tearing.

With no more interruptions, she finished and gave the shredded paper pile a toss and turn. Unzipping one of her jacket pockets she produced a fifty pence coin and a bright pink disposable lighter and with both in each hand she readied herself. She took a deep breath and waited.

If anyone approached the toilets from outside she was sure she would hear them. Failing that, the opening of the main door would warn her.

She unlocked her cubicle but kept the door closed by lifting her left leg and placing her foot against it. She picked up a piece of torn tissue from the pile on the floor and flicking her lighter, lit the corner of the paper. Immediately it caught.

She lowered the rapidly burning paper onto the pile where it began to catch and ignite the other scraps. Placed on the ceramic tiled floor she knew it would not burn for long and there were no other flammables within reach to cause a major blaze. That was not her intention. The torn papers on its own would burn out soon enough and serve its purpose.

She promptly got up and left the cubicle, pulling the door closed behind her. Using the 50p coin in her hand she inserted it into the outer lock's centre pin groove - designed for emergency access from the outside. Twisting it, she heard and felt the bolt move. The indicator showed red for engaged.

She had practised this many times with these very same doors on numerous visits to the gallery.

No one entered the toilets as she executed these steps and leaving the ladies she saw the lobby was empty. On opening, this part of the building usually took a while before it got busy. The two guards at the desk were still absorbed in their excitable conversation.

Directly in front of her was the brief set of steps leading down to Gallery A that she had checked out earlier. Without delay, she descended them.

Emerging into a large open-plan room she noticed one guard in a corner slumbering on a chair. He looked up briefly at her and then resumed staring down at his shoes.

Another was patrolling the room with silly looking strides. Other than an amorous couple whispering in front of a particular painting, the gallery was quiet.

Appearing to be late for an appointment, she marched through the myriad collection to the other side and the exit there.

Then the klaxon of the alarm bellowed out. The automated female voice announced that fire has been detected in the building and instructed people to leave immediately via the nearest exit. It had been less than five minutes since starting the blaze and now it had been detected by the sensors in the toilets. She acted quickly.

Outside was a swinging staircase that led up to the main gallery floor and on her right a fire exit. To her left an elevator which she approached and pushed the call button. The door pinged opened straight away.

Checking no one had yet come running through, she leaned into the elevator and pushed the button marked 2 on the panel and held the door from closing with one arm. She then clenched her other fist and using the underside of it, struck the plastic covering of a fire alarm positioned on the wall.

This second alarm would cause more confusion to the control room and floor staff. There were now two emergencies in the gallery that had to be dealt with and it was these distractions that she was relying on.

Releasing the obstructed elevator door, she ducked inside. The door closed and the elevator began to ascend. She took a deep breath.

The door dinged open on the main floor and the cacophony of the alarm bounced around the rooms. On her left people were already moving hurriedly towards other exits in the building, away from the supposed danger. Gallery staff could be heard nearby urging, informing the fleeing and panicky public to safety.

On her right a corridor of small rooms were already emptied. Directly in front of her and opposite to the elevator was a quaint desk and chair set in an alcove. Adjacent was a labelled fire hose reel cupboard and opening the four foot panel, she climbed into a larger interior the size of a small wardrobe. Crouching next to the reel she pulled the door closed behind her.

The attire she wore was chosen for this very situation; loose fitting clothing which would not hinder her movements in the dusty and cramp space.

Almost immediately she heard running footsteps approaching outside and the elevator door opening. She suspected a member of staff was checking the elevator was clear of public - part of the evacuation procedure until a voice was heard to utter impatiently 'C'mon now. Get out of here.'

She cursed inwardly. She'd been rumbled!

'Alright, alright! I'm going.' Another voice answered irritably.

Then she heard two sets of footsteps retreat and fade away. She heaved a silent sigh of relief.

Crouched in the cupboard she remained. Tilting her head slightly, she was trying to detect any other movements or persons nearby amongst the prevailing racket of the alarm.

She slowly pushed the cupboard door open and carefully eased herself out from its confines. Looking left and right she saw the corridors and adjacent rooms vacated and wasting no time, she nimbly entered Room 26 whilst pulling out of her inside jacket pocket a short rod of metal. Measuring about a foot, it was in fact an extendable pry bar.

On the left wall of the first room was a 'Nicolaes Maes' interior and without delay she began to work. Extending the pry bar, it doubled in length and using the fine flat edge she was able to easily slip the bar into the narrow gap between the wall and the hinge of the painting's frame.

Crude as it was, there was no better tool for the job. Made of titanium it was lighter than most tempered steel and just as strong.

Now with a small cavity pried apart, she was able to wedge the rod further in behind the metal hinge and get the leverage she needed. She then grasped the pry bar's curved end hand grip and pulled. Not much exertion was required, the hinge popped out of the wall's plugs like a cork out of a bottle.

She repeated the procedure with the other hinge.

The emptiness of the rooms and the continual siren only emphasised the riskiness of what she was attempting. She counted on the alarm drowning out the wrenching sounds of the working tool.

Suddenly she heard running boots approaching her vicinity but whoever it was fled pass the corridor unaware of her and what she was illegally undertaking. Whether it was security or public they were oblivious.

Far off she could hear the raised voices of staff communicating with each other over the repetitive bell. At one point too close for comfort, someone yelled 'It's clear!' That confirmation brought no reassurance and she knew much still depended on pure and simple luck.

So effective was this crude tool, she had the painting off the wall in less the thirty seconds.

Moving quickly she left the room the way she entered with frame and painting under arm and pry bar in one hand. She pushed the elevator call button and the door opened straight away with its now familiar ping. It seemed to sound louder than everything else but it was only her usual trepidations that played on her mind in tense situations like this.

This job was different, nothing like her usual 'modus operandi.' Despite that, her homework had been done.

Inside she pushed for ground level and as the elevator descended, she retracted the extendable pry bar by pushing one end against her stomach and pocketed it inside her jacket. She then placed the 19x16 inch frame into her prepared Cass Art bag, covering it with some rolled linen canvas.

Another ding announced the opening of the elevator door but it did not bother her now if its sound drew security to her presence. From here on, her body language and expressions had completely changed. She was breathing heavily; out of breath and a look of frightened bewilderment pained her face.

She turned left and ran for the fire exit doors. Passing Gallery A, she noticed it empty and then she was pushing and banging with her fists, kicking the door in feign frustration and fear until she finally pushed against the bar that activated the door's mechanism. She crashed through the opening doors and seemed to stumble and almost fall into the body of a security guard standing by outside.

'Thank God!' she screamed hysterically. Sobbing she grabbed onto the man like he was a lifeguard. 'I thought I..... I thought I was gonna stay st... stuck in that lift. Be burned alive.' She was stuttering yet she didn't give the guard a chance to speak. 'Sorry I'm ash... as... asthmatic.' She was heaving erratically, her body almost falling from his supportive grip. 'Thought I was... was... was gonna die in there...'

The security guard was clearly troubled by this panic stricken lady and held her reassuringly. 'Are you okay madam. Do you need assistance?'

'No... No... Thank you. Thank you.' She continued to gasp. 'I'm fine. Out of that... that inferno.' She exaggerated.

Worried that she may faint on him the guard did not let go of her. Her cumbersome bag bumped against him but he barely noticed it. Her safety was all that concerned him.

'I thought my colleague had cleared that section. I do apologise madam.' The guard apologised. Perturbed by her 'inferno' remark, he told her it was only a litter blaze and nothing to be alarmed by.

Another member of staff and some solicitous members of the public that had been congregating nearby had approached. 'You're safe now love.' Said the other guard and the public observers nodded their heads in reassuring agreement.

She stood on her own two feet now and with a heavy sigh uttered 'I'm okay. Thank you.'

The guard no longer held her but still concerned, he watched her.

She brushed her dishevelled hair from her face and began to assert herself. Her panting began to subside and she seemed to regain poise. She nodded to everyone in the group 'Okay' again and again. 'I'm fine. Fresh air is all I need now.'

The two guards satisfied the distressed woman was okay returned to their positions by the entrance to the building; continuing their duties by refusing people entry until the all-clear. Two Fire Engines blocked the road and Firemen were busy manning hose pipes and entering the gallery.

Gradually she moved away, appearing to all purposes embarrassed by the whole episode. Composing herself she noticed the guards and public interest was no longer hers and eventually slipped away unnoticed around the corner of the building until she was back in Trafalgar Square.

She was now no longer wheezing, out of breath and frightened; in fact the complete opposite of a damsel in distress. It had all been amateur dramatics of course and to her satisfaction it had worked.

The front of the gallery had become an evacuation Fire Point where huge crowds of gallery staff and visiting public congregated. Nearby was a Caffé Nero and crossing the road she entered and ordered a large Macchiato. While waiting she swopped the weighty Cass Art bag onto her other shoulder, easing the burden.

Carrying her hot beverage she strolled back into the square and here she leaned on a wall by a plinth and while seeping her Macchiato, lit a cigarette. She took the stolen painting off of her aching shoulder and rested the bag carefully between her feet.

She watched the impatient tourists and the sea of uniformed staff loitering and waiting around for the gallery to re-open. The sun shone down from the blue and white but there was still a slight chill of winter's end.

Twenty minutes later she noticed staff being let back into the building. The all clear had been given by the Fire Brigade. Her deliberate decoys had been dealt with.

Fifteen minutes later beverage finished and another cigarette smoked, the gallery was re-opened to the public. They briskly poured back in, almost emptying the square.

This was her cue.

Cass Art bag back onto her shoulder, she began walking back towards the National Gallery. She entered the Getty entrance and strolled through the bright capacious Annenberg Court looking to all and sundry like any other visitor and lover of art but she was actually carrying one of the National Gallery's paintings.

Reaching the Espresso bar she turned right making a bee-line to a staff door situated at the right of the seating area. Here she produced a pass and swiping it on the electronic panel reader, it beeped green and she pushed the door to enter. She swiped her way through two more security doors - it appeared she had complete clearance and access - and made her way down a corridor of offices. Two members of staff passed her but not one approached or questioned this stranger until she arrived at the open office door of the Head of Security. She knew this place only too well.

To this day she could not believe she was back in this building after all that had happened but it was beyond her control. The then Deputy Head of Security had cottoned onto her. After being questioned again and again by the police for days afterwards, she had believed she had gotten away with it but he had her followed and approaching her revealed what he knew. Uncannily, he had ascertained her motives when she had concealed herself in the role of the Head's secretary. She almost admired his guile - he was an ex-policeman and still ambitious. If she returned the diamond she had procured from the gallery's vault that night and performed one job, he would not divulge his information to the police. It was blackmail pure and simple and she had no choice.

Entering the acquainted office, she strolled up to the Security Head sitting at his littered desk and taking the Cass Art bag off of her shoulder placed it upon his paperwork.

He had short trimmed greying hair and an immaculate sandy beard. His face conveyed someone who had seen it all and did not seemed perturb by this abrupt interruption to his busy schedule.

'You need to revise your security arrangements.' She declared with a self-satisfied statement. 'That was far too easy.'

The Security Head gazed up at her with congenial eyes. Looking inside the Cass Art bag, he smiled knowingly and replied 'Thank you Ms. Ellis.'

'You know that is not my name.' She said.

'But it is because of that that we are here. Wouldn't you say?'

She didn't answer him.

'You've cut and dyed your hair.' He remarked.

'I can see why you got your job.' She said sarcastically.

He grinned with amusement at the comment.

She placed the security swipe onto his desk. 'This is yours. Are we done?'

'I appreciate what you have done.' He genuinely meant it. 'It makes my job easier and yes, you're secret is safe with me.'

She eyed him with mistrust, nodded reluctantly.

He leaned back in his chair, stretched his legs. 'You know, you're talents are wasted. You could use your skills in a more noble vocation.'

'So could you, you bastard.'

She left the office with him chuckling to himself.

Afterword

Originally the pseudo-thief was a guy and I thought it would be a little different to have a female. I then realised this was Hannah - a character I had already written for in my novel 'No Die For Gold.' That's when the ending changed dramatically to what I had already envisioned.

For all those still crying out for a follow up to that much enjoyed adventure; call this a teasing sequel of sorts!

With that, this succinct story wrote itself within a few days.

April 2016

GALLERY SLASHER

I enter the Sainsbury Wing. Picking up a gallery plan from the information desk, I don't pay for it and proceed up the grand bland stone staircase.

I was a breath of fresh air in all the grey. People's faces lit up and smiled at me in my dazzling brocade. I was dressed in fine Oriental garb - an embroidered satin Chinese long red dress with a dragon and phoenix design and a Mandarin collar; a traditional gown that draped to my feet, where a pair of red sequins twinkled like Dorothy's. I also carried a jasmine Cath Kidston bag. My hair was a black bob, long fringe over a deliberately unflattering pair of spectacles that made my brown contact eyes big. To round of my disguise, I wore what was common to Eastern travellers – a surgical mask and white cotton gloves.

I was pleased with my appearance of a sweet, innocent Oriental tourist. I was revelling in the attention despite it being counterproductive to my purpose here.

On the main floor which housed most of the collection, I strolled into room 9 and then room 8 where like a china doll I delicately placed myself on a wooden bench opposite two Michelangelo's.

Still people gazed at me and my exquisite apparel and in character I bowed a dozen times only for them to contagiously bow back. At one point I had to wave away a group who attempted to take photos of me. I couldn't allow that.

I looked at the unfinished paintings but my interest was the adjacent room 7. As I discreetly watched, visitors came and went while the guard inside stood sentinel.

Opening my Cath Kidston, I pushed the gallery plan inside and wrapped it around the object within. I then pulled both out and gripped the plan which concealed my accomplice.

Soon the guard left, replaced by another.

Getting up, I glided over and entered the room as a couple were leaving. The room was empty except for the guard.

The intimate space contained only half a dozen paintings on the four plum coloured walls. A faded blind covered a window above where the guard sat on her chair. She was a short plump young woman with long chocolate brown hair tied up into a ponytail. Her tiny feet didn't quite touch the floor and her legs dangled.

She glanced up briefly as I entered, revealing round spectacles on a dour face and then resumed playing with her phone. How rude! How could she not acknowledge my beautiful attire?

I briefly perused the room with feign interest but eyed the two exits. I then decided there was no time like the present.

I approached the guard and in a squeaky toy voice said 'Excuse me?'

I couldn't resist throwing in a bow too.

She looked up uninterested and from within my gallery plan which I still carried, I withdrew my shiny friend. With one well practised swing of the arm I slashed at the guard's upturned and exposed throat. Her eyes were still vacant as her head lolled forward. Blood began to spurt from the sliced wound. Splashes of red on the guard's white shirt and crimson pointillism on the floorboards.

There she remained perched on her chair, already dead.

I briskly left the room – my dress swishing in my hurried pace to leave the building. Halfway across room 9 a piercing scream shrilled throughout the rooms. Someone had discovered my handiwork. My masterpiece.

Murder had been committed in the most iconic and public of places.

The National Gallery was now tainted in blood by my hands. Ha! Ha!

I felt untouchable and powerful. The glee coursing through my body at what I had done was intoxicating.

It felt like a 'finger' to the establishment too and it would be an embarrassing and shocking wake up call to the powers that be.

Initially the building was evacuated under the ruse of a potential fire hazard and eventually closed for the remainder of the day when the severity was realised.

Not at all privy to the procedures, I knew enough to know what it would involve. I had seen and read enough of that most saturated of genres on TV and in books. Crime scene secured, forensics, witness statements and CCTV footage would be collected. Everything would be examined and scrutinised in detail and all manner of investigated tools would be utilised. But still they would not catch me.

I imagined the consequences of my act playing with the minds of the staff in the building. I, the antagonist of their fears and they completely unaware.

The gallery re-opened the next day releasing a statement denying murder had been perpetrated on the premises but it wasn't long before they had to admit the truth. Multimedia and the internet had a way of leaking the facts.

There was always one witness or clown in the loop eager to talk despite the gallery and police insistence to all involved not to divulge any information in case it interfered with their investigations.

The press began the merry-go-round circus with headlines or scoops becoming a commodity regardless if it was genuine or fake news. Social websites were soon ablaze with rumours and speculations with every Tom, Dick and Harriet providing condolences, opinions, theories and angry tirades with each other and the world.

Terrorism was mentioned even when no fanatical groups claimed it was their work and I guess that had to be expected. I felt somewhat peeved though that my handiwork was deemed something commonplace as an 'act of terror.'

The plan played out like a dream. The killing felt so natural. The simplicity of taking someone's life was as easy as blowing out a lit candle and this was only the beginning. Security would be stepped up but it wouldn't make no difference. I had more people to murder!

The slow entry into the gallery was due to the bag-searching that was now in operation and had been since my first act.

I was a patient man. I had to be considering my intentions. Like many places since 9/11 the threat of global terrorism had become every day. Airports of course, train stations, tourist attractions and government buildings all had security aches in place as well as every person subjected to searches. It was only a reminder of the reality.

In front of me in the queue, a group of French school kids hustled and bustled in matching plastic yellow backpacks. They picked their noses and scratched their crotches like teenagers at a concert.

I was attired in a long green Moss Bros tailored coat, striped white shirt with a lapis lazuli tie, Alabama clay coloured cords and smart brown Hush Puppies. My crisp grey Fedora was pulled down low over my Oco Grandmaster tinted glasses. I also carried a brown Aspinal Attaché briefcase and on my hands, a pair of black leather gloves. I wore another wig – this time a mass of black perm. It had an unnatural sheen to it but I hoped it would look like it was matted with hair products. I also wore a fake beard – the best of its kind and very convincing. All of my face was covered with the wig, the beard and the sunglasses. There was nothing recognisable about me in my killing attire.

Before long I passed through the doors with the heaving throng. In the lobby two bouncers stood at a table ushering the French kids in as quickly as possible without a search. The whole operation wasn't exactly thorough. Most visitors were told to empty their pockets into a tray and walk through the security arch. Occasionally the machine emitted a beep; the guards sighed and gave a brief wave of the security wand. Buttons and belt buckles were the usual suspects.

At the table I went through the motions like every other pleb; emptied my pockets of wallet, keys and coins. None of this stuff was mine of course, they were just props.

I opened my briefcase and the guard perused it contents. As well as the newspaper, pens and mints; I threw in a couple of porn rags. Couldn't resist it and I enjoyed the look of embarrassment on the guard's face. Classic!

Briefcase and possessions in the tray I also placed my hat on top of my case - this was important. The guard nodded and with a hand urged me through the arch. He still had no idea who I was? Only yesterday, we were neighbours in the rooms and I had even given him some gum! The wig and beard were doing the job and I proceeded to walk through the arch without a buzz.

Purposefully I walked through the airy space of Annenberg Court bee-lining for the Espresso Bar where here I sat myself down on a stool at a breakfast bar. I had no intentions of ordering anything – at these prices!

I faced the lower galleries which were adjacent and watched people come and go.

Ten minutes later, a gallery guard entered and shortly after another left.

I waited a few minutes then got off my stool and headed into the lower galleries myself.

In the first room, a young ginger haired guard sat on his chair writing in a notebook. Continuing on into the next room, it was empty and on the left another room, another guard – an older gentleman dozing on a chair.

Straight on into the last room I entered and the female guard here turned her attention momentarily away from a very large painting to acknowledge me. Her face frowned, unsmiling and she had ridiculous bright pink hair. It was Crazy Sharon and she hadn't recognised me.

Also present was an elderly female visitor perusing the collection.

I sat down on the wide wooden bench in the centre of the room facing the same painting and placed my briefcase by my feet.

The reason for Crazy Sharon's rapt attention was Delaroche's 'The Execution of Lady Jane Grey' but occasionally she would look back around her room at the other visitor and myself. Her expression continually morose and her arms defiantly, defensively folded. Her uniform blouse and skirt were stretched unflattering over her lumps and bumps.

No other member of the public came in and soon the elderly visitor left. Sharon turned her head to notice this, a brief glance at me and promptly returned her attention to the painting.

I picked up my briefcase and placed it on the bench next to me, opening it. The snap of the locks was loud in the quiet space and Sharon turned her head and eyed me with more annoyance than suspicion.

I mumbled a deliberately undiscernible 'Sorry' without revealing my true voice and still she was oblivious to who I really was.

Her annoyed eyes which always scowled warned me before she resumed what she had being doing ever since I came into the room.

I removed my Fedora and retrieved from the inside band, my shiny friend. I replaced my hat on my head.

I caught a glimpse of my grinning self in the mirror like blade.

I took one more glance back out of the rooms - I could see all the way down to the exit and Espresso Bar - no one was coming this way.

I took three nimble strides towards Sharon, my knife flushed with the side of my leg. I am right behind her when she hears my deliberately heavy breathing and she begins to turn her head.

I swiftly bring my shiny friend up and around to her front and exposed neck. I smell her soft strawberry scent and sliced her larynx.

She immediately clutches her throat – they all do – as her blood began to spray through her fingers. So was her inability to breath or even shout.

Crazy Sharon fell to her knees in front of me and keeled over.

I notice blood had struck the satiny dress of Lady Jane Grey. Under the bright lights of the room, the painting had a remarked vivid and surreal quality to it. Dramatizing even more what had befallen the short lived queen.

I had already stepped back and thrown the knife into my briefcase - so swift was my slash, the blade remained unbloodied. Snapped shut, I left with my suitcase and still no one entered the room.

The dozing guard next door – Mr. Thompson - still dozed. The ginger haired guard Andy still scribbled. And both unaware that I had just murdered their colleague. Ha! Ha!

The media went to town with the story. It was now global. The internet abuzz. Everybody had something to say and none of it novel.

More and more officers were brought in. All staff were going to be questioned. Motives supposed. CCTV footage search would also encompass the streets of central London. Inevitable but futile!

In books, TV or the movies you always hear the rote proclamation that to catch a killer the cop must think like a killer.

Well how about: To elude the cops, the killer must think like the cops!

I had plenty of time on my hands to be meticulous with every detail, every eventuality. Back up plans from A to B to Zee if necessary and played them out again and again in my mind. Everything I rehearsed would lead to the perfect crime.

If my colleagues were frightened before, now they were terrified. The uncertainty bred many rumours and one that put the nightmare in them was that the 'Gallery Slasher'- as the media termed me - could well be one of them. Ha! Ha! They were right without ever really knowing. It was I and I relished what I was doing to them.

If colleagues had to make a list on who they would like to see leave; Crazy Sharon would have topped it. Well, she didn't have to now, she was dead and she wouldn't be screwing around with people's lives anymore. Scheming, manipulating, lying and sucking off people like a leech! She was a vile person and her fat trap was finally shut.

I could almost hear the good riddance chorus! Ha! Ha!

My first victim was Moody Marie - she was on that list somewhere.

No longer would we have to put up with her miserable mug. She carried cynicism like a cross and we all had to bear it. She used religion to belittle others and better herself. I had to put an end to her sanctimonious bullshit.

They were all dead before I killed them. The dregs of society and I had to work with these degenerates. Put up with their black bile that spewed from their crooked mouths. Their brains worked less and failed to function. They lacked decency and empathy. Breathing and wallowing but never swallowing.

There was talk of walking out. Well of course there was, my blood-works the cause of it all. Ha! Ha!

The Union stepped up, declaring the working environment was now a hazard. Ha! It could not be more dangerous than death! Some staff simply didn't turn up for work and a handful quit without a 'bye' or two months' notice. The guilty ones perhaps?

My colleagues were running scared - faces like deer in headlights. Now they had a genuine reason to procrastinate. I saw and heard all the fear pervading their awaken minds, distressing over every move they made. Oh so cautious in what they now said and did, lest they're actions would make them next? Ha! Ha!

What a wonderful pantomime and all my doing. I walked among them unsuspected and overlord!

I entered via Orange Street, the usually quieter entrance to the building when school groups were not running amok.

Security was tight as the Queen's bedroom and bag searching as intensive as an airport. There was no sloppiness now. Every visitor was thoroughly searched. It had a knock effort too as queues stretched around the block.

There was a much larger staff presence as well as Police and PCSO patrolling the building but all their precautions would make no difference whatsoever. I would murder my third member of staff and nothing in the world could stop me.

I took much satisfaction from dressing up in the costumes and I admit it was an extrovertive side to me that I revelled in. I liked them all but there was something about this one that I got a real kick from. Maybe it was because I was attired head to toe in a black, diplomatic Burqa.

There was nothing distinguishable about me but the bright yellow M&M bag I carried, declaring in its tacky brightness that I was yet another tourist. But a Muslim one at that.

I knew this was the reason I felt aroused. It was taboo! Being an disbeliever of any kind of religion and wearing this attire was no doubt disrespectful and I thrived on the controversy.

Both my black bum bag and M&M bag were searched and then placed into a tray which was pushed to the other side of the table. As instructed, I walked slowly through the arch without emitting a beep.

My search had been much briefer than others were subjected to and I had hoped that my wearing a Burqa would go in my favour. Not wanting to offend, they hastily passed me through. There was a brief moment where the guard gave me eye contact between the narrow slits on my headpiece but it was only glancing and I was not recognised by my eyes.

I could see how I could be suspected but also respected too. This was only a figment of what it was to be Muslim.

I walked up the stairs being careful not to trip or stumble on the abundance of material on the Burqa – it was huge like a bed sheet!

I was now in the North Wing and I spent half an hour pretending to peruse the Dutch collection before heading into the Sainsbury Wing.

Here I walked halfway down the stone staircase to level one and the ladies toilets. In one cubicle was a maintenance panel set into the back wall. Opening it with a 'pocket utility' key, I reached down into the dusty confines and retrieved my shiny friend which I had securely taped to the inside two days ago. Into my bum bag my knife went. Ha! Ha!

I composed myself and leaving the toilets, proceeded back up the staircase to the main floor and this time I turned left into room 51.

Here there was an alcove of sorts; a smaller darker room that was often overlooked by visitors which housed Leonardo da Vinci's rare work 'The Cartoon.' I sat opposite on a small bench set into the rear wall.

Five minutes later the building's tannoy announced that the gallery would soon be closing. I had timed it perfectly.

An influx of visitors began. Coming and going, eager to see everything else before the closure.

A male guard frequently patrolled; waiting for the room to empty - I had done it a thousand times myself. He was Christian, my next victim.

He had black hair and a black beard and his dark eyes always starred seriously, giving him a brooding demeanour. Why was I going to murder Christian? Because he was a bully! Far from being a Christian himself, he was no different to the rest of the trash. He used his six foot three to intimidate and oppress. Bludgeoned people with his presence, telling them what they should be doing and what they shouldn't. I wondered how he would stand up to my shiny friend.

There was no way he was going to recognise me under this Burqa. Why would he and with the room's lights dimmed low – not a chance.

In the shadows I removed my partner in crime and holding it, clinched it behind my back.

Christian came back into the room to check it was clear – it was empty of public alright and eyeing me, approached. Without knowing him, you could see in his body language that he was about to bully me out of the room. But before he could ask me to leave, I struck.

Standing up, I brought my arm around, raising it to his height and with a swift glint of polished metal, I slit his throat.

I moved aside as he fell forward, incredulity in his wide eyes. His hand on his bleeding throat; the instinctive reaction was to grab me with his other hand. Whether it was to stop his fall or a futile attempt at apprehending me, I was not sure but he missed, stumbled and caught the M&M bag I carried, tearing it from my grip. It ripped down the side of its thin paper material, the individual bags within bursting.

Momentarily I am taken aback, surprised as hundreds and hundreds of brightly coloured M&M chocolates fall, bounce and scatter across the floor.

Christian struck the bench and somehow stayed slumped against it.

I was somewhat mesmerised by the sight that covered the room's floor. Even in the dimmed lights it was a kaleidoscope of colour. M&M's and blood akin to a Jackson Pollack.

The dead guard remained where he was collapsed against the bench, his legs curled up beneath him and his head buried into one of his arms. To all appearances it looked like Christian was praying and the irony did not go amiss on me. Ha!

I shook my head of the reverie and made my escape. Not running but joining the rest of the public being urged to leave the closing gallery.

They would never catch me.

My time in the rooms was not wasted starring at the walls, procrastinating and complaining. Over and over it played and I edited it like a story.

And this was only the beginning. There was a whole bunch of reprobates to murder.

You may think me foolish. That no crime was flawless. That I would eventually slip up, get caught. But in my mind, I was proof of the perfect crime. Ha! Ha!

And that is why they would never apprehend the 'Gallery Slasher.'

In my tediously boring job as a guard in the rooms, what else is there to do but daydream all day?

Afterword

'Man does not make ideas. Man's ideas make him.' Not sure who said this?

This started as a short simple crime story before it grew and grew and potentially became more and more tangled than the imagination of a bored guard in the gallery rooms.

The original draft could well be the basis for a novel.

April 2017

head Pitch

"Right, okay… Okay, ready? Clear that hectic head of yours Andréa. Here we go…, this is it."
He was standing with arms spread theatrically like this was an audition. Well it was in a way but he would never be given an Equity card, not for all the money in the world. An actor he was not.
He bellowed like an un-credible Brain Blessed. "Viggo Mortensen is……"
There was an over the top, un-dramatic pause,
"………… John the Baptist's head."
There was a silent stampede of tumbleweed.
He waited keenly, rather tickled with himself.
She stared back at him with one eyebrow attempting the high jump.
"Is that your pitch?"
His raised arms nearly amputated themselves.
Rhetorically he cried "You don't like it?"
She resumed chewing gum, her jaw doing cartwheels.
"Sounds distasteful Costa."

"Ah, come on."
"What's with the head?" she apprehensively asked.
His reanimated arms flapped but it was his tongue that gave flight.
"Okay, okay. Right, it's coming…." 'Sell it boy, selllll it.'
He loaded himself with glorified glory.
"The title has it, it's the money shot Andréa. It's the hook that will make the public curious. And of course; Viggo Mortensen, an established name. Unusual name too, striking and bold. He's a mix of a young Richard Gere and an experienced Daniel Day Lewis and he is leading man enough to put bums on seats. The ladies love him right? His manly good looks and ruggedness; they practically get wet panties over him…."
Her expression said, 'Not for me he doesn't.'
She obliged him some more freefall.
"Okay…, so John the Baptist, a big, big name from the Bible. I mean he was Jesus's right hand man for God's sake…."
He was oblivious to what he had actually just said but she still felt like throwing her gum at his sweaty forehead for that pathetic quip.
"…..Everyone knows the Baptist right. That would bring interest okay. We need a new Bible movie. When was the last one eh? Anyway, there's never been a film solely about him, John the Baptist. Why not? Gotta be some bucks there. The church should be up in arms about that. Hell, they should be funding me….."
'If he utters another pun I will throw him outta my office, via the window and straight down to hell.'
"….even that name on its own has to be a power draw. The Baptist, like say, The Terminator or even better The Godfather." All the 'The's' were empathised like bullets.

They were blanks to Andréa as she still chewed her herbal gum like a nonchalant cow with cud.

"The head bit, no one expects that okay. They just presume Viggo is going to play all of John the Baptist but no…. it's just the head, his head. John's head being played by Viggo's head…."

All these raps about heads were giving her a headache.

"…. and that's easily done with some CGI okay. Don't even need Viggo's body. So no costume needed there then right?" He was grinning like a joker high on the juice. "Just film Viggo's head reading his lines and CGI it to…."

"WAIT!" She barked, as the plasticine gum skidded to a stop in her mouth. "You say the head will be talking?"

"Yes." He said it like it was any given Sunday.

"But John the Baptist will be dead?" she tried to comprehend but failed like a zeppelin without air.

"Yes and no. The body will but the head not. I mean the body don't even figure, okay. Well maybe very briefly at the beginning to show where the body is at…and at the end in completion. But it's all about the head…."

"You keep saying that."

"That's the point Andréa. It's the MacGuffin."

Costa Jacobs was the Max Bialystock of the Writers Guild. Being called 'Loser' as often as the hours didn't deter him one iota. It only blindly careened him on like a headless dodo.

How he could still remain a credible member of the Guild after all these years was as baffling to Andréa as adults without kids buying tickets to see Harry Potter.

A screenplay short he wrote eight years ago (about a zombie that wants to be a caring human being again) was passable even with the help of countless more rewrites; a film that was hastily made and just as quickly fell straight into the DVD's down and out dollar bins. Not only was it a flop but it would be known as the movie a film critic first penned the phrase 'slop-flop.'

Since then all his scribbles were about as interesting as the diary of a full blown dyslexic talking about a bout of diarrhoea. His trashy stuff was so far down the tether that he was just clinging to used toilet paper. He made Ed Wood scripts seem like multiple Oscar winning magnum opuses.

"It's original." He deemed.

"It's obscene." She rebuked.

The gum in her mouth felt like a pebble now. She took it out and wrapped it in tissue and she then swivelled around in her carousel chair and threw the gum into a hungry bin like a gold medal depended on it.

'Bingold!' She congratulated herself.

It was her made up name for this game.

She certainly did have a lot of spare time on her mind some days. The moniker was an amalgamation of bingo, gold and bin. It summed up what this moronic pastime of hers was all about. The clever use of these words once made her gloat but lately though she would berate herself for being such a dumb bitch, wasting time on such an infantile distraction. It was all a restless reaction from the days when it rained here in Hollywood and when it rained nothing ever got done. That weather just dampened everybody's ambition. No one came, no one called. All the opportunists stayed indoors incommunicado, watching Oprah and stealing plots from Murder She Wrote.

There was a box of cigarettes snoozing on her barren desk, she awoke one and planted it between her rouge lipstick lips.
Lighter alight, she droned "What's the plot?"
How many times had she run this shtick question only to sigh 'Why? Why?'
Yet she had to let them bang her eardrums with their pointless pitches. It was a tough job but…'no clichés please'…, she was ice queen.
Well, she certainly couldn't be nice like an ice cream in this job.
She yanked opened one of her desk draws and began tapping cigarette ash into it.
Occasionally like a good fuck, a script would land on her desk that was rococo to her reservoir ears and beneficial to her shoe bank.
"Well he wants his body back." He baa-ed sheepishly.
Her eyes rolled like marbles behind the smoke, pulling on her cigarette like she was sucking the last of her favourite milkshake through a straw.
"Costa darling…" The nicety was nefarious. "You got to give me more than that. I don't deal with sound-bites."
"Okay, okay…. Sure there's more. It's coming." He fidgeted, heavily.
He had to sit down before she blew him away. He swore she had a revolver in one of those desk draws.
'Make the most of it Costa's fat arse because the way this is going, you won't be sitting for long.' Her psyche sharpened a machete.

The office always looked like it had just opened that day for the very first time. Everything in it was brand new asylum sanitary, so immaculate bright white that you felt you needed sunglasses and seroxat to remain safely and sanely in the room.

Only a few items were trying real hard to look commodious on her white altar like Formica desk and everything else was cowering orderly away in invisible cabinets. Minimalistic had nothing on this die hard space. It was a rightful refection of her personality; bleached and neurotic. The office warned fastidious worked here, 'So, go ahead, make my day.'

He felt like she was eyeing him as the one and only filthy thing in her office. Well, to her he was!

Overtly broad in the beam, bald, pink and perspiring like an abattoir pig in an unflattering tent like creased and soiled suit. He looked about as comfortable as a live lobster realising he was about to be sacrificed to the ravenous in a boiling pot of water.

Andréa's work life and private life were two different lives rigidly and religiously kept apart. Like Jekyll and Hyde sharing the same straightjacket but taking turns.

She was Italian as spaghetti and married to the critically acclaimed and critically panned film director and pasta sauce maker Antonello Machiavelli della de Jacometto or begrudgingly 'Ant' to all and sundry but his mother.

So happy were they in their twenty-six year marriage together that they both shared that happiness bounteously in numerous affairs. So utterly devoted that they proved it every day, unconditionally by constantly arguing and fighting with the passion of two proud bulls cloaked in red.

In this nullifying industry of movie making Andréa left a taste in every client's mouth like rancid meat that had been marinated in urine.

Yet it worked for her.

She had large blatant cosmetic surgery lips on a roadkill face and a voice like a chainsaw and always dressed in Inquisition red and Reaper black.
She was once described by her priest as a devout upstanding catholic and a monstrous agamid.
She idolized her priest; Father Vader and the schmaltzy attention she drooled upon him at church and charity functions, you would think he was the Holy Spirit himself.
She also coveted his cock.
Of course she knew that that was blasphemous but 'even the most devout get tempted sometimes, that's why we had confessional boxes' she told herself. 'All was forgiven when you confessed.'
Even the carnal urge was too much in confession sometimes. With Father Vader in the opposite box listening to her made up sins; she would shove her hand down her panties and begin to play with herself while she listened to Fathers deep sensual voice praying for her. It truly released her urges, those purging moments.

She was waiting - a predator with a perm.
It was now or never thought Costa, the final push of the pitch or the best fucking begging in the business. He run with it like a giant boulder was bearing down on him.
"Okay, okay Andréa my angelic agent. Imagine abstractly, metaphorically, spiritually of course because that is the gist of this story that John the Baptist's head is…"
"Would you stop saying that?" She spat the interruption. "Just call him John for Christ's sake." She fidgeted like a wingless fly. 'Merda! Now he has got me saying those insipid puns.'
"Okay, right, will do. Okay…. So John….." She was giving him the Medusa eye with a 'don't you dare.'

He didn't dare pretend he had the guts. "….is on a quest, a journey to find his body. Why? Well, you see, he is haunted. A ghost if you like, in limbo and the only way he can get to heaven is he must be buried with his body too, both parts together. You know the catholic burial rituals that decree a ticket through the pearly gates so that you can finally be laid to rest, in peace, in one piece. Right?"
She knew it alright as she stubbornly stubbed the cigarette into her draw and un-gently closed it. 'He was romper stomping on sacred ground here.'
Scrutinising him like a Black Widow, she baited him "Go on……"
"Okay, so we have the archetypal antagonist King Herod. An evil sprout of an evil root as the Bible tells us. He was the son of the elder Herod who was the slayer of the entire first born at the time of Jesus's birth. This is all interesting stuff Andréa. So Herod will be the bad guy, he's the goon who ordered the beheading of John, right. Okay, the female lead will be Saint Johanna. Now she was married to one of Herod's steward, you see she was a servant, so there we have a rebellion from the lower class, more intriguing stuff. So she rescues John's head from the dung heap it was thrown into according to the Bible and originally buried at Mount Olives okay but I've written it so that she reunites John's body; that was buried in a tomb by the disciples, with his head. So she…"
There was a tremor from the phone on Andréa's desk. "Sshh! You talk more than me and I'm the agent."
She barked into the receiver "Agents are angels." Her usual declaration; All her callers were well aware of its rum sarcasm.
Listening, she began to inspect her nails with her stainless made to order gnashers. "Yes…. Yes….. Yeah... No. I will

not…… I won't…. Look, did I not say no? Yes…. No. Ciao." She replaced the receiver.

"Bastardo." She called the phone.

Costa winched.

"C'mon Costa, get me convinced."

Once again she yanked open another drawer, plucking out a rabbit food-filled homemade Panini. Unwrapped, she began nibbling at it like an anorexic squirrel.

Costa jump-started again with all the restraint of a runaway train.

"Okay…. So Johanna, the servant girl not yet a saint of course, will aid John on his crusade. She's freaked out at first by this floating head, this aberration but she eventually begins to believe in God and the whole working in mysterious ways thing right. Other characters from the God book pop up too….."

'Characters! God book! BOOK!' She started to seethe. 'The Bible is not a book, like some cheap Mills & Boon or Dan Brown novel. How dare he! And he called these sacred individuals characters, like they were made up in one of his substandard screenplays. Sacrilege! It's Gospel and HE IS taking it in vain.'

She was biting her tongue as well as the food in her mouth. He was trying her tolerance, testing her commandments about never mixing her work with her personal life. She wanted him to feel her wrath. 'Count yourself lucky atheist a-hole.' She restrained.

"….It's got a lot of potential elements for a great film, compelling sub-plots. The scope is Cinerama Andréa. Biblically epic, could be award worthy…."

'Yeah, the Razzies if you're REALLY lucky, cretino." She was bubbling like a sarcastic volcano.

He was only able to still babble on because she was now consuming her Panini, not at all like an anorexic but an Augustus Gloop bigarexic.

"……It goes back to the old Cecil B. DeMille movies of the halcyon age of cinema and at the moment the Academy love post modernism twists of classical literature right……?"

'Literature! Is he saying the Bible is literature? Oh God, I've only got the one tongue. Give me more patience Lord. And Virgin Mother Mary too.'

"……It's got it all, even comedy too…"

Her eyebrows raised like allied gun turrets on advancing Nazi death squads.

"Well light-heartedness, okay." He pacified pathetically.

Andréa portrayed psycho.

"Listen, I got this scene based on the Bible passage where Herodias, Salome's mother, pieces John's tongue with a needle after his beheading okay. That happened too. So, get this, he has a speech impediment when he talks with Johanna."

She scrunched up her nose like the putrid undead had just waddled into her spartan office.

"Why Viggo?" she mumbled through cheeks that were bulging like a hungry hobbit.

"He's got that uberman quality. And his eyes. Have you seen his eyes? They got empathy and compassion, just how I imagined John the Ba…." He quickly braked and abruptly U-turned…., "…John had that. The Bible conveys that. You ever see that painting by del Piombo; the daughter of Herodias it's titled. John's head on the platter looks just like Viggo Mortensen's, I swear it does. It's Viggo's head Andréa, dead ringer… Ha!" He couldn't help himself, the satire possessed him. "That's funny….." He smirked like a corny gremlin.

Panini consumed, Andréa expertly rolled the wrappings with her witch like fingers into a ball and threw it towards the waste basket.

No 'Bingold' this time, it fell to short.

She growled like a bored teen wolf with a chip on her shoulder.

It bothered her.

He bothered her.

Costa pondered why someone so meticulous about cleanliness would have the bin so far away? Maybe it was a game for her? Well she lost that one.

He gave a smug look and regretted it.

Clawing open another desk draw she pulled out a small bottle of green liquid and drank of it in thirsty gulps like a vampiric Bacchus.

Her schizophrenic eyes danced to and fro the wrappings and Costa.

It was a stand-off.

Costa was only too aware she had to make the move.

She feigned indifference.

Then got up, moved swiftly, jerkily like an arachnid, plucking up the wrapping and dropping it into the waste bin. She was back in her chair again like grease lightening.

Costa pretended to not notice like someone who wouldn't spot a real dinosaur in Day-Glo pink dungarees pounding down the street towards them.

He quickly began pitching again like he was shot putting above his weight.

"It's looks exactly like him. It is that painting in the National Gallery that inspired me to write this script. It has to be Viggo, no one else for the job. De Niro too well known, right. All you would see is the great De Niro, not the Baptist. And Cruise, well he is just too clean, still too young looking. I mean he would still be perfect for High School Musical; he still looks like a brat, okay. Caprio, well I love that guy. So, so underrated, but just not got that mature, wisely face. Not quite old enough yet. Viggo's the man. Gotta be."

'This has GOTTA BE stopped more like.' She exhaled. "Sounds disastrously like a madcap B-movie to me Costa."

"Well, okay…. Okay a bit of both maybe, but it can be so much better, right. Look at it like this Andréa, it could be a B movie tribute at its best. So good that it's an A movie. Hollywood loves the originality of Indie movies that they could only dream of making. But they are stuck in the black hole matrix of making the same old re-tread blockbuster garbage right. The Gordon Gekko complex of film studios."

'This loser has been watching too many movies.' She thought. "What ARE you blowing about?"

Costa could have had ears the size of Dumbo but he would not hear.

"I can even see some kind of tag line for this…." He was in that eighties deep voice over mode you heard so often trying to make a crap movie sound more exciting then 'Orgasm; The 3-D Interactive Movie but really it was just an empty popcorn box.

"The Good, The Bad and John the Baptist's Head."

"Not good." She said ugly.

He was the kid running with a red balloon.

She was the antagonist waiting, hovering with a pin.

"I don't know yet but something along those lines okay, it's a work in progress that the producers can sell right.

Okay, we throw in a few humorous lines like you only need a HEAD to be baptised. Or John was Jesus's HEAD disciple. What about…." He halted.

Because he was slowly being turned to stone by Andréa's iceberg glare.

She lit another cigarette.

"Okay, okay… We can work on the jokes."

Resistance was futile. "No." She gave him the ten second warning.

"Okay. Well stuff can be….."

"No." She alerted at 'five.'

It was inevitable.

He feebly fantasized like Don Quixote that all he needed to do was move the needle on the record.

"Okay. Can I leave my script?"

She snatched that metaphysical needle with an explosive screech and burst his metaphorical red balloon.

"It's not OKAY, right. And I'm not okay. OKAY?"

With desperation, his dying, squeaking helium voice lamely reached for the stars… "Got this script about Russell Crowe playing the angst-ridden Eddie Vedder, the front man of the Seattle band Pearl Jam?"

With the subtle diplomacy of Genghis Khan she said, "HEAD…" 'Oh the irony!' "…for the stairs Costa." Beautiful she revelled. 'That's appropriato line if ever I heard one.'

Deflated, he got up and began to mope his way out of the office like a plimsoll pressed spider.

'There is something wrong with that woman.' He mulled.

He attempted to slam the door with enough impact to cause Armageddon in her office but failed that too as the door was on a slow moving spring hinge.

Venomously and sarcastically, he imagined writing a screenplay about a compulsively neurotic female Hollywood literary agent who has always got to have some kind of substance in her offensive mouth…..
Gum, cigarettes, feigned food, potion drinks, nails and cock.
"Bitch." He confided to the staircase.

Afterword

All though this story does not actually take place in the gallery, it is based on a painting IN the gallery. And although written over six years ago, I was encouraged to include it in this collection because it was considered amusing.
I hope you agree.
November 2010

THE DARK SECRET OF THE NATIONAL GALLERY

Did it ever strike you our visitor, why there are so many nationalities employed as security guards in the illustrious National Gallery of London Town?

From all joints and jaunts of the globe, we bring sugar and spice that will enhance your visit and in some very exceptional cases, we will go above and beyond the changing of the guard to make it an unforgettable experience.

If you haven't had the pleasure, come in, visit us and peruse. Marvel with kaleidoscope eyes at all the captivating and iconic paintings and I guarantee you will ingest a thing or some. You may even be surprised at what you already know or recognise, buried deep beneath all the paltry, poxy and day to day distractions piling up in your psyche.

Do approach the gamut of guards too. We are not disparaging or dismissive of you in our responsible duties. Chat with us, enquire. We are expedient, engaging, eager and bored. Your interest and converse is stimulation for us, it relieves the endless day. But do make sure you leave before closing time. It could be a stain, a pain, a sinking 'Bismarck' on your visit.

We are empirically the United Nations here and our employment has nothing to do with diversity of countries or cultures though it certainly appears that way. Nor a deliberate design to accommodate all our visitors from around the world with flagging flags and torpid tongues of familiar fellow compatriots.

We have a much shadowy and loathsome recruitment process here without the rigmarole of prosaic interviews and months of scrupulous vetting for suitable candidates. Our distinct method dissects all the time-wasting. The post-shredded tête-à-tête prostituting posturing and the pleading petition self-sell interviews.

I should know. I found out the grim and gruesome way; the dark secret of the National Gallery.

This is a visitor announcement. The gallery closes at six pm. The security staff will start closing the gallery at five to six, the shops at quarter to and the toilets at five-fifty. The National Café remains open to eleven pm....

The anticipation begins.

Our hearts begin the bass pounding drum roll, akin to first night nerves backstage before going on, though we have been doing this for years. Us pro's, darlings and drama queens treading the gallery boards for centuries, just like our familiar's painted portraits that hangout on the walls like extras on a background set.

In here, time beats sluggish. It's not of the norm this limbic limbo. We have our own absolute anomaly clock that co-exists inside each of us and we are unable to ignore its tick-tock oscillations. Nor can we break free of its cog like cuffs; no more than you can escape your inner voice.

The last half an hour and hope of possible release will drag akin to the longing of adulthood from green youth. Yet we somehow, someway remain on the verges of forbearance.

Compassing our rooms, cavities like caged animals. No bars but a farm here. On stalked heels we are eagle eye-balling our quarry. Lips are gnawed lines, nails are filed with egg tempera teeth and exhaustive sighs filled the air like pollen.

It's the same at the end of every shift, as we all avert our lingering and langsyne pupils from the bodily masses that may or may not be the last to leave the floor, our fields.

It wouldn't do to stare. We do not want to encourage them anymore than we had to – well, not at any rate. Invitational eye contact could reveal our veritable motives. We only want them to leave – well not all of them at any rate – to be gone from our agitated and sanguine presence.

Aloft, the 'big brother and sister' CCTV is our audience and the watchers know only too well what to expect. Like regurgitated replays, they've seen it all before as they observe the ghostly images being exorcised from the house. Who will stray and is that a big bad wolf lurking in uniform clothing there?

We couldn't be seen to be grazing and gazing too long. Not to cause uncomfortableness or inordinateness. We do not want to put the frighteners in them! It could be our undoing. So no hasty flapping amongst the foregathering flock, we reprimand ourselves.

We watch each other nevertheless. Observing the mirrors of much to be desired in each of our bloodshot eyes and keeping each other in check as we wander and squander through a nonspatial continuum.

Slight perspiration surfs on our palloured skin that lacks air and sunlight. We spend most of our lives here akin to the antiquated in their last home, the quiescent, quenching place. Daylight a distance we have almost forgotten yet agreed in its absence. The feeling past like spent synapses. Day and night we are sleepwalkers here.

'Obiter dictum,' it's often been commented by wannabe judges how we all look enviably vernal for our ages when the more curious discover our eon-lasted existence. The oldest of us could pass for twenty or thirty years younger than the truism.

It's the building itself. It preserves us. That's why the rooms themselves are so climatically extreme from one to the other. One colossus kiln, one tower block refrigerator: A domain of inverse climates in a contradicting continual flux; the humidity and the wintriness, the sulphurous with the cold-blooded. Each varying temperatures like laboratory levels and test tube conditions. Uncomfortable to you our guest, we apologise but ongoing to us living features and fixtures; a pain in the neck.

As we skulk through door after arch, it's a slog out of the mad dog desert and a slip off the edge of sandpaper sand into a bitter North Pole dead of the night.

These inordinate fluctuations are not only for the protection and longevity of the collection. It preserves us as well as the centuries old paintings. Us the elite are just as rare too.

We had become the same in a sense. Brothers and sisters adopted and adapted to the material. The doors are our windows frames, the lamps undying stars and overhead our protective heavens. We are cocooned in an ersatz bubble of inhabiting and vegetating. An oxygenic preservative drip feed. This is our existence!

The gallery will be closing shortly. Please collect any items from the cloakrooms and return all audio guides. The gallery will be open again tomorrow. Thank you....

It is intensifying now and we just want closure. Lock the building down and set us free from the fasting monotony.
Numbers are dwindling; it makes our end of days easier.
If you look, scrutinise us closely, you may notice the recondite penetrating pupils that seem to stab right inside you as if we can behold your vulnerable biology, what makes you throb!
Also the advertisement licking of the lips that portrays appetite of what's being sold and a palpability of what will be bought. The hankering and panting becoming unbearable to some who want to purchase but spin in impatient and increasing circuits of our accounts. Shuffling like the aimless and unspent undead.
Our peering and appraising becomes leery like, looking bodies up and down akin to horny intoxicated boys or dirty and desperate degenerate old men. Or even an unfussy dog eyeing up potential succulent scraps; a piece or a drip surmount to a plate or an overflowing bowl. Grinding, sharpening canines in a premature, ejaculated, dribbling expectation.

More and more people are vacating – opportunities lost, perhaps? The rooms emptying - decorative tombs and suited coffins and we linger, remain like sterile sentinels. Ancient Jackals overseeing our treasures, ourselves!

We wait for the signal, prone while our minds concoct our twilight. What is to come to pass this evening? The excitement is tangible in our manic smiles and we are ready to jump down and run with our glee! In the flight of fancy we are escapees from the institution.

Listening ever so keenly, it's like peering with ears perpetually popped and antennae pricked. We hear everything; the rustling of worn out dead animal skin and the flaps and falls of feet; characteristic of whom they are, their DNA echo, footprint. Whispers too of conversations and conspiratorial murmurings like scuttlebutt spirits - air conditioning sea in a shell.

Keys, many keys swaying and jingle-jangling as if they grew on plantations. These were all the resonance of closing; the annexing, eviction of bees from their hives.

In our heads, the tsunami of rushing blood to our temples. Veins, rivulets in our temples pushing fore-lines on a living live map. The adrenaline was narcotic, heroin.

The radio crackles, the voice cackles and the booming holler of a town crier that is the team leader bellows 'Gallery closing.....!'

Can you not hear the Fairground bells! It's what we've been waiting for all day. All our lives for today! Oh the joy to come!

The call reverberates around the building like a howl, embodying a cry, a triumphant guttural roar from the very bowels of our voracious stomachs. We just want our supper!

We become a pack of wolves and if the public could articulate our inner utterance they would scarper high-tail to hell - it would be a better place!

We are baying insanely, insatiably. Provoked, we kindly and patiently like condescending care-workers ask them to leave the premises. Abstract animated windmills, we encouragingly waved the direction to exit, when truth be known, we are rubbing our hands together in a salivating song.

Our prey is being urged, herded by our swelling numbers.

Loose wheels of Joe Public deliberately slow down; pulling over but there is no lay-by here. You can see their defiance, their scurvy attempts at becoming immovable hubris objects but they move because pride is a bride to the fallen.

We are silent in numerous languages and dogged in our strategically positional presence. Subtle artifice, eat your heart out!

There is a stiff-necked, reluctance still. We like those ones and thus kick our heels. Maybe tonight, we get to purge our dissatisfactions.

There would always be one flavoured fool, one fully paid up member of the pineapple club. Stubborn, pompous and assaying a stand akin to a primary Baboon in front of its troop. Beating his chest mechanically, the machismo as inescapable as the 'I' in id.

The issue worthwhile was only for awhile - spilt milk a splash in mediocrity. An infringement of their rights was only contradictory. 'Rights' are only 'rights' in the right place.

In the end, the rocking horse would buck them to the ground or the soapbox they squatted turned to suds - it made no difference. Their static protests fell on blood thumping perforations. Though they couldn't grasp it –

simply too simple for the simpletons. All they had to do was leave but no, they face the faces. We, the gallery of masks in this ancient hallway!

Like alligators in the street, we move the sweet meat public along slowly but surely. Sweeping our tracks we meet more of our esteemed reptiles on corners. Always keeping our fodder in front of us, fore to the paw! No one left behind, no residues or remains.

The portraits window the walls. Always watching us disapprovingly down their template noses with their stern headstone faces. But they remain silent as they know only too well. They have seen our souls. Witnessed our work. Seen this unspoken recital, ritual all too often and like reluctant and pious priests in confessional boxes they cannot confess the terrible deeds. Abetted in their silent guilt; they are accomplishes.

We nod our heads like undertakers and with inaudible footsteps continue rounding up the lost or leaden.

In the main hall now – not dining but circling the last stragglers and coaxing them down the main staircase in a doom like death march. A funeral procession with our drooling chins six feet under.

Eyes furtive yet conscientious not to reveal our true 'fleur-de-lys.'

A uniformed congregation; simpatico we respect our pickings and one in particularly that strikes and sounds in his peacock-ing, promising.

You can see, hear and sense all his obvious and oblivious resistance. He defies us with a hollow discharge of disregardful words. Holding up hands on a fat fashionable watch – yes, it's our time, not yours. We own the clock idiot - and strutting his newly white feathered 'FCUK' t-shirt which is basically a base 'fuck you.'

It only piques us. We dare you, you bastard!
We begin to goad him by answering back with the recorded, pre-programmed reels and spools of rules and regulations like a stuck record.
He portrays the holier than thou slant that is all so stock and for game we play parlance without the words like a cat would with its food. Toying with our cotton-ball prey, this was our turn, our 'comme il faut' after all the faeces thrown our way. Insulters, inebriates and imbeciles watch out! This is payback for being a 'shit hit fan' all day.
We could not err, we were within our courts and our numbers made our lines. We remained dug in trenches while advancing and digging deeper into their spaces.
The fool could not catch sight of what was to come. We had something to pitch and throwback. Yet he persisted with his futile protestations about our closing procedures and it made no iota of difference to us. Endured it all before on our old weather beaten shammy leather skin.
Now he realised the overwhelming odds stacked against him, the more our numbers multiplied, the taller this wall of waifs loomed. Sensing defeat he began to fabricate, lie and spit untruths and insults like a spoilt immortal. It made no sense to us anymore; we were ignorant like our illiterate guest, foreign to it.
We would be doing the world a service by shutting him up and shutting him out. What was but another appendage of brainless nation amiss and not missed? We were redressing the equilibrium karma of common sense in a world overran by suits with no sense that led the half-wits and were as welcome as dysentery.
So we bedevil some more, rile him and rule him in.
Though he spoke in clipped English, it may have well been gobbledegook. He was Italian with a souped-up Vespa

voice and he hands sawed the air like an inept juggler. He didn't know it but he was offering himself up like a willing sacrificial body.

He was beautiful though but weren't they all. A 'Zoolander' with one of those faces and bodies which was all that they had going for their existence - independent thought not required. What more did a Michelangelo marbled feature have need of? His skin was olive oil painted and delicious. I couldn't stop fixating on him, he a feast of a delectable form. My loins warmed with stirring carnality and my groin tingled for touch. I imagined him naked and me daubing all of his physique with kisses, licks, love-bites. But my heart was as heavy as a pair of 'Lover's Balls' because I knew I would never have him. That all I would have after he had gone would be a masturbating moment.

I was surprised he was on his own. They usually grazed in hyena like football squads numbers. Invulnerable in their entire wet black designer clothed mannequin forms. Dominating, invading like their Roman forefathers.

He was young and cocksure and immediately reminded me of myself. Those days before my rite of passage when no one could of told me what to do. I was as headstrong as arctic tundra, believed the rules did not apply to me and respect was spiel that the infirm establishment propagated. I finally understood back then in a baptism of fire what I was and what I was not.

I became liberated in Legion!

All we can hear now are the drums thumping louder and louder, faster and faster. It was the pulse! The universal rhythm of life and lust! A growl rises in us from the dungeon deep part of our gut. The beats like jolts of currents in our veins. The 'sinus node' of the heart conducted from our beating bosom with its rousing orchestra. A speaker itself on full gain and reverb. The pulsations could literally been seen twitching in the flesh of our proud chests. Trying to burst out and dance, sing, scream, grab and feed. Run amok!

There would usually be one who wouldn't leave until the final turn of the deadbolt. This was him!

The idol Italian, the last remaining member of the public in the building. The masses have been pressed out of our premises, spilling into the square like ants and once again under the crush of the city.

He was on his own now and unaware of it because he still berated to deaf ears, there was too much of else for us to bother with.

The guards, gargoyles on the doors locked the last with a bass and a satisfying tinkle of the nethermost ivory key.

We have our victim. Alas and ruefully in this case, in all his 'bellezza' we could not adopt him. It has already been decided despite the empathic and helpless romantic in me wanting this Adonis as my mate. He was not to be an employee this time, not this strapping stag. He would not be one of us but only sustenance. The protracted wait, the aching, wanting in throes had without words pre-ordained it. I knew ever since I laid my misty eyes upon him but it made the impending loss no easier and despite our exteriors and posturing, we were not without love.

He was aliment to our immoral needs.

Blood lust boiled over with our silent howls and febrile fervour.

We eagerly, hungrily pounced.

The release from mortal etiquette, a needle to the arm.

'Ciao Bella.' I silently, stupidly prayed for him. We weren't without our gods too.

None of us refrained, I admit. The ravenous and frenzied spell swallowed us and we quenched the thirst. Consuming the deity's drink!

A colleague immediately went for his throat. Sinking his teeth and silencing his larynx. His screams should not be heard.

The blood hosed us and our laundered uniforms darkened like litmus paper. The lobby became an abattoir floor.

His gaping, death-rasp mouth silently screamed to the uncaring. His eyes reflected the unearthly horror and ordeal.

In his death throes and thrashing, we gorged. Taking turns and well-mannered queued for this macabre buffet. Tearing him into greedy, desperate peel like pieces, we sucked of his delicious dripping tasty flesh. Even slurping and licking his blood off the cold marbled floored plate like thirsty Lupines. Nothing was wasted but bones to be discarded afterwards. When we were sated, full and bloated, we saved bits of morsels to chew and draw on later.

The reprieve is always worth the wait.

Our hunger was over.

For now.

You can now see there are no prejudices here.

Every nationality is welcome.

Any fool can join the National Gallery.

Afterword

Zombies and vampires seem to be everywhere these days. Why not the National Gallery!

May '15

THE PLAYGROUND

There's no place like home, well our second home if you will and unlike Kansas, nothing quite like it. No red shoes here, we wear only regular issue non-descript black and there's indubitably no clicking of twinkling heels. It's more a dragging of heels.

What sets us apart from many - if not all - of the other parallel establishments of ol' London Town is how institutionalised we still are. While every other tourist mecca has modernised profit wise, we still have a stubborn semblance of Victorian current and conduct. Somewhat archaic but nevertheless 'sui generis.'

Let me invite you through these dormitory doors and hallowed halls to the institution and its inmates. Family and friends, inane and insane, the fuckers and fiends.

There is nothing to be revered here. Nothing so sacrosanct. You will only discover a playground and all of its children, schizophrenic with love and hate.

Not even in the building yet and she is looking for an exit. Dilly-dallying outside she pulls on a cigarette like she's sucking through a squeezed straw and itches for an affiliate.

Boring Noreen reminded me of the portrait of 'Margaretha de Geer' – Rembrandt's 'Dot Cotton' if you will.

Note from here on readers, I will allude to colleagues with a particular painting that has some similarities with themselves. I can't be naming names. How unsporting that would be of me, I actually like most of the reprobates.

She leeches onto a familiar face and follows me in. In an abbreviated way possible she asks how I am but really it's all about how she is. Akin to Cocks yodelling in the crack of morning, she needs to be heard.

A 'Good morning' or 'Hi' is acknowledgement and enough for me. It is not an invitation to tell me all about the colour of dog shit she trod in earlier OR the smell of the stranger she sat next to on the delayed train journey in. It's too early for chit-chat and I don't endorse a conversation.

'Talk later' is misunderstood. She seems to think its talk now. It's too early for platitudes and probably forever.

She gets in and wonders what she's doing here? Not even started and she's finished. Already defeated, the attitude is anathema.

Not the best way to embark upon the day.

The boy's changing room; no different to school days and locker-room mentality. Albeit there is a lot more grey and girth limping about here with pseudo war wounds. They almost believe they are soldiers the way they grimace and bear their crosses. They see time in the rooms as a 'tour.' All gums not guns a blazin!' Braggadocio bravado and bullshit bickering. Belittle-men in actuality!

Young or old it is not long before the floorboard trenches wear down your gallery issues and you're as weary as the well-trodden path.

Coughing, spluttering, sneezing and heaving like a London Fields' pub. Jack the Lad chat and exerting testosterone in all the presumptuous plexus places. Next they will be comparing penis sizes!

I've heard its worse in the girl's locker rooms. Bickering bitches! So a little bird twittered me.

Clocking in with grumbles, comrades begin squabbling over their positions for the day; anything to avoid that Piccadilly Circus position or that infantile individual. Or a hankering to be next to their pretend best friend. It's akin to 'Top Trump' cards but with rooms.

Why couldn't they do what they were given? Warm their derriere and watch people like they watch the box. It's all soap!

They see the same fugitive furniture and fittings – paintings blurred to wallpaper and if you did not like who you were next to, well you were not obliged to faux pas!

Could you imagine this in any other job?

'Oh Sarge. I've swapped with Banks. I'm on mess duty and he's frontline. That alright? Pretty please!'

And so you witness those canon-fodder faces that could not get out of the denominated duty, un-resigned and slumped in the corners of rooms and scowling at all like cantankerous juveniles.

They set themselves up for the day like 'Jack in the boxes!'

Talking about 'wind-ups;' that is Nicolaes Maes 'portrait of Jan de Reus.'
With the same old stoner face and smoking grey hair, his voice was a rasp and breathe injurious. Good laugh but sometimes didn't know when to stop. Gregarious like a chimpanzee on crack and like one of those energizer kids that tells the same joke again and again because it was so fucking hilarious the first time.
He had a good attitude though, didn't take the job too seriously and fair play to him because play he did. He certainly made it an interesting experience for the tourists and I'd say meeting him could well be the highlight of their visit. The gallery's Court Jester if you will!
Colleagues jibed that he was on drugs. Well so what if he was. Whatever got ya through the day and at least he wasn't a sourpuss!

There we go, that's the call. The floodgates are open and soon the pilgrims will be treading the tripper-mill.
Then a sound like car-breaks, Boring Noreen passing through the rooms blasting her horn about her positions for the day and how she has no one to talk to. She still finds a way though.
Colleagues tend to bypass her around the building like motorists avoiding potholes. She just jolts and jars you and in the face of the familiar highway signs, you are never road ready for her.
There is some tumble-dust in the corner of my room that's needs my upmost attention and she reluctantly chugs on with a world weary sigh to her room like a child to the naughty step.

She will be gate-crashing you all day long like a road-rager!

Once you settled in the rooms, you can relax. The hardest part of the working day is done. Getting up and getting in. Sit down and loosen-up now. Watch the congregation come and go.

The employment itself did not require a lot of employ. More a boondoggle slug! And it is important to stay positive in the vacuums of the rooms. We are often on our own while the world and its neighbour blurs past. The threshold old, sleepwalking days and a day dreamer's haze. We are in a private world of our own in public.

Occasionally a visitor will amble up and ask a smug question in the lines of 'Are you bored?' Or 'What do you think about all day?'

To the former, the answer is 'I'm bored of questions like that.' And to the latter, it's 'Sex!'

Whatever you do in the rooms is most of the job done. Your 'there-ness' is all that's needed. Like a scarecrow in a field but can point in the general direction. But it is, that the easiest job in the world had its pitfalls - doing 'fuck all.'

Don't fall a-kip! Some nod off standing in the room akin to a donkey in a field like our very own blot on the landscape Dinosaur Dave.

Over the years staff had been caught in the rooms slumbering and for the repeat offenders they were fired. It was the cardinal sin!

If you spent your entire time sitting and couldn't be bothered to get up and lap your room a few times then you were plummeting for the drop off. Do what you have to do. Pacing and panting. Scowling and ranting. Daydreaming is not dozing. Socialising and scheming. Reading and writing.

Scratching or biting. As long as you did not succumb to sleep. Stay awake, whatever it takes.

Really, your presence in the room is enough. So pick your nose, chew, fidget and fart but find something, whatever, that gets you through the day.

It is all about time too and for some there never seems to be enough of it to know what to do worthwhile anyway. Mock Minutemen scrutinise clock faces while others pick at an imaginary hair under their chin. I couldn't think of an easier job, except maybe a sperm donor!

Time and motion, rhyme and notion, it's all the same. Move from one position to another posterior. One, two, three, four, easier then walking through an open door and if you cannot remember those rooms then you may as well get a brain transplant.

And still they get lost in a circle. Follow it around and you can only end up back where you started 'super-sucker, damn fool fucker!' Don't know where he is going but we are all following and if you are incapable of getting back on time then stop doing the sums 'Bob Hope.'

See that guy hopping by like an errant emu and burying his head in his hands? That is del Cossa's Vincent Ferrer with even less hair and even more pained features.

Loved the job so much he bought it home with him and like a marriage it screwed with him. The job stressed him out so much that it rewarded him with a five star breakdown. Poor chap did not help himself when his whole life was a set of spreadsheets and commands. So undermined was he, he finally crashed. The program Vincent Ferrer could no longer process under such utter rhetoric and contradictions that the gallery seem to run on.

But don't worry, he would eventually turn himself off and then back on again. You can't keep a first class fuckwit down!

Now there's nothing wrong with taking pride in your work but if you're looking for a pat on the back here, you better be ready for the sucker punch! Why put yourself out when you will only be hung out to dry.

The undermining was legendary in this institution. From the underpaid cleaners to the overpaid Director, all had experienced the sour taste of the proverbial custard tart in the face!

You know that old adage – 'you don't have to be mad to work here but it helps.' Well it couldn't be more in alignment then this lame academy. Those that joined sane, took to it with gusto and became certifiably punch-mug. If you're not careful, thick skinned or roof aloof, you too will end up counting the floorboards or talking to the paintings.

It's a mad house here. Inmates of the institution. Don't let 'em out into the real world, keep them incarcerated in these cells.

If you're inclined to gibber yourself than it is already too late. You thrive on that like an addiction. You know it's no good and it screws you up but you just need it, crave it until its carving you up inside like a junkie's carvery!

There's 'Bartolomeo Bianchini.' Chews gum like a camel and speaks to himself. Or maybe he actually has an imaginary friend?

Observe him long enough and you notice he never sits. Or maybe his seat is taken by his imaginary friend?

If you are lucky, you can get more than a mumble out of him that passes for conversation. That is when he's wasn't having a discussion with his imaginary friend. Though it's all grunts and groans, shoulder shrugs and suspire with the habitual 'God willing,' he usually spoke about the Company and its monumental miscarriages.
Other than that he is quite content as cement and gets on with the job. Maybe the only thing that gets him through the day, is the company of his imaginary friend?

This colony will affect and inflict you no matter how 'blasé supreme' you may be because the regurgitated atmosphere pumped around and around the air-conditioning always comes back and gets under your skin. Just like your colleague or neighbour, permeating your body and mind with their malaise. Anyone who dons the uniform must be prepared for the parlance and the pantomime.
The best of us, the bereft are only drops in the big yellow tea-pot. All ingredients of this stirring tepid brew.
The balance of play-performing and faux-socialising is ostracizing at its worst. An imperceptible line and you are guaranteed to trip over. Because this quagmire undermines all and sooner than later, no matter how uninvolved you protect yourself, you are spun in encroaching circles. Going around and around each bend of its corridors like characters down the rabbit hole.
I've got a bird's eye view and I grounded on my seat.

Room to room and what it entails. Or the lack of it.
Our day usually involves a quartet of rooms or positions. One rounder's of these and you break – well some have

already broken but I allude to 'tea-break.' Another round and it's lunch and finally once more round the bend for an afternoon break. At least it was musical chairs - years ago you were given one room for two weeks. What ornamentalism that must have been and colleagues complain about what they do now? You are spun as much time in the rooms as the cobwebs!

It was more regimental back then too, akin to a boot camp without the obstacle course - just your gallery issue boots actually. Needing the toilet you had to be touching cotton and if you chatted, you were marched out of the building before your gallery issues touched the floor.

If it wasn't akin to a geriatric institution then, it is now. We eat, drink, piss, shit and mumble indiscretions all day.

Inevitably you are drawn to a quasi-professional query about work by a noisy neighbour and more often than not it leads to the true M.O. Gossip and gripe and all that garbage they have a need to imbibe. It is all quite rum and lacking the spirit!

There is a whole heap of waddle waffled and repeated too like senile retirees. Inane chatter akin to a pneumatic drill and as palatable as poo! They hear it, so they believe it.

Uncomfortable with stillness or their own company they fill the space between their ears with even more boring baloney. It's like being cooped up with chickens and a whole lot of clucking!

Six o' clock is a long time. A sentence to some! They crave the company of diversions to get them around the clock. Anyone will do; wannabe celebrities, plastic personalities, cardboard cut-outs. Even Boring Noreen will suffice.

Glancing at your time pieces as often as the bat of an eye. Time ain't gonna go any faster if that's all you do. Think you are killing time? No, it's killing you! Stop staring at the face that only stares back. Reminding you of time wasted and you wasting away. It conveys the emptiness of your existence. The paintings have more life!
Silent silence and the loneliness of the short walk only remind them of their worst. Asking poor questions of themselves and answering poorly. An idiot's inquisition!
The workplace, the only place where they are just a shell of their former self. More than just a uniform but a little like monotony man!
It's those with the narcotic need, their sudoriferous coming down. You spot them prowling the rooms hungrily for garbage and going cold turkey for gossip. They loiter by doorways they shouldn't go through. Akin to scavengers prowling for scraps. Yet unlike vampires they need no invitation.

A cackle prangs into my headspace. Boring Noreen informs me she's off to the loo. I need to know that like I need a crown of thorns.
For some, toilet breaks become an opportunity to sort out their affairs – make calls or visit the post office. Some simply grab a snack or sneak in a smoke and usually taking as long as they possibly could. And the team leaders can't say anything to them because they go boo-hooing to the Union.
Instead of having a piss they take the piss.

Platitudes – trite, humdrum or obvious remarks. Staleness of thought or language.

Everyday platitudes bore me. And that is all a lot of people talk about. As if the act of socialising is based on bloody platitudes. Filling noiselessness with wish-wash, a need to offload oral offal. A form of verbal masturbation.

Traffic, trains, strikes and the cross-dressing of seasons. Like para-phrasing parrots, it is all been said before. Rote until it becomes a blank record. It is banal, boring and I would rather experience root canal. Its leprosy of the tongue!

Excite, provoke, and fuck me in conversation!

But most don't, can't, because they can only do fucking platitudes.

And when I throw something unexpected into the mix, they look at me like I said the world is flat!

They are the plebs of platitudes.

Don Andrés del Peral. About as talkative as toast and when words do come, they are mumbled like a kid with mumps feeling sorry for himself. He is the spitting image of Goya's painting right down to the crestfallen mug. Worked here for an eternity and still has no bloody clue where many paintings are and gives information like the Cookie Monster. He had the appearance of a homeless person and was the longest standing piece of furniture.

He worked with one eye opened and is mostly left alone like the hard of hearing granddad. And that is what we are, a clan of sorts with all our baying and baaing black sheep 'an all. The familiarity has its faults and if there is any folly, it's inherent within themselves, hereditary just like families.

The jealousies, insecurities, foolhardiness and tantrums all stained on worn sleeves. Kiss and make-up, make-up, never do it again. But they do, they can't help themselves.
Don't take it so personal my porcelain dolls, its only work, something to hold down.
Allegiances change as often as the rotations. Moods like the moves that push you from room to room and mode to mode as long as you have someone to justify your existence. Someone to lend an ear that you can bend! Someone else to blame!

Talking of black sheep, here's one to avoid like a black hole. She sucks the patience and positivity of even the most pious positron. Unlike others, she had no resemblance with any of our portraits. In fact the 'Ugly Duchess' had nothing on whom was known as the 'Madonna of Malice.' It wasn't so much her appearance but her personality was as pleasant as the plague!
She connived and lied. Took pleasure from taking other people's pleasure and was as rotten as that 'way past its best before date' apple in the cart. People tended to keep a quarantine's distance – colleagues and public alike because she had the air and aura of an electric chair. Like her soul, her hair writhed and curled like snakes. So don't even glance at the Medusa my friend. Move on! Stone has a habit of being stuck between a rock and a hard place.

Time to march on, my next post.
That's AK-47 Kevin. Don't give him one whatever you do. We would all be very afraid!

All he talks about is weapons. From air guns to surface-to-air missiles and some say he is dangerous to know. All I know is, I don't wanna know!

He looked like Lucas van Leyden's 'Man aged 38' who in turn resembled Frank 'Oh Betty' Spencer. An accident waiting to happen one day, AK-47 Kevin will bite off more than he can chew of the foot in his mouth. That is, if he hasn't shot himself in the foot first!

He leaves the room faster than a Scud and generally points under the chair where the panic button is and usually never is. Lost? Or in his pocket? No one cares?

Talk about how negligent they are about this important tool…. Okay I may be a little pedantic here but they are crucial.... Alright, maybe they have A use. When THEY ARE working! When they don't, you may as well be calling the council!

Some colleagues treat them like novelty key-rings where the novelty wore off five minutes into the first day on the job.

There is almost always an ingredient of shirking in most jobs and 'de rigueur' there's not much ducking and diving is in the easiest job in the world. Yet still they bark about light in daylight! Clearly they have not the capacity to be content and ineptly they do nothing about it. Set in their ways but fail to see they are not set in concrete. Lead boots and shackled minds come to mind. All talk and no walk.

Well there is a lot of walking but it is always back to square one. What they've always known. Home base without the run! Day in, day out, zone out!

There's a wearisome tenderness to boredom here and the only thing missing in all this self-deprecation is slippers.

Contentment is what is lacking for most and that's a consequential difference to complacency. With contentment there's some joy but not with this lot. There about as cheerful as cholera!

And no one complained more than Psycho Pete. Spitting image of Guercino's St. Gregory the Great but without the greatness and as volatile as Vesuvius. Blew his rag and like the poor victims back in that infamous day, you don't wanna be around when Psycho Pete pops!
His posture was decrepit and his body language conveyed a pending demolition. He didn't do eye contact as if he was afraid he would see the godawful truth about himself in your eyes.
He sees red like we see black and white. His temper is Tempest! And has been known to destroy things while internally he's slowly combusting. It is only a matter of time before he implodes and then what will we do for entertainment?
The damned fool can't help himself. Let's a lot of shit inside build and build and cannot let it go. No matter how many times he paces the room, these futile laps go in circles, ever decreasing and derailing to his own private hell. He has no release valve, where is that steam gonna go? Pop goes the psycho!
How much does it cost this time? Just another apology probably but who's going to keep paying for the unhinged doors and crumpled 'wet floor' signs?

Pass the buck, ride your luck, who gives a fuck! Shuffle-board the problem around the system.

There were some who made it extremely difficult for themselves. The easiest job in the world and somehow they would dig themselves a hole. It should be a walk in the park that is the playground of the National but they approach it as a war zone. It's as difficult as you wanna make it fool!

They stomp about with bother boots but it is all inaudible footsteps. Watchful eyes that seldom look at anything – it's all see-through. They manhandle what is easily handled. Minor becomes major. Saving face by making faces.

There's a lack of self-awareness and neon hindsight and only they have themselves to blame for their self-made 'schadenfreude!'

Why the attitude when it is inevitably anathema?

Cancel the power-trip too, that road is bumpy. If the approach is off, you're gonna land in the rough. Overt exuberance despite your better intentions. More like cortical immaturity.

Why you want to shout at someone for a minor indiscretion when it is only going to get a boomerang to the barnet!

It's almost like they want the confrontation and I wonder why? A need to be seen, heard, felt by an unimpressed audience or managers who don't care and don't what the hassle. Hackneyed hubris? Taking out personal grievances on Jill & Joe Public?

Lose the leash and give some lee-way. No rule here man but the ruse. Whatcha trying to prove? That you're in control? But you ain't no got no groove. Un-judicious man! Go with the flow and float with the flotsam!

'Ear, ear!' Boring Noreen invades my ear and she's still two rooms away.

'I just found out I won't get my weekend bonus because the Christmas holidays fall on the weekend.'
'But the gallery's closed.' I point out plainly as the coral nose on her face.
'Yeah but I still lose my bonus.'
Can you believe that, I tell myself and I answer the rhetorical with an affirmative.
Good luck with that one 'Boreen.' Why don't you suggest it to the Union? They could pass a motion and flush it straight down the toilet!
There's gotta be more to life than money and it's a fucking holiday she is still getting paid for. Seriously, there's gotta be more to this void.
These are the miser where money is their God. Screwed like regulars Scrooges they are! Their avarice no different to the 'tax collectors' in that painting by van Reymerswale and just as ugly.
I turn my back on her greediness, her neediness and her hullabaloo.
Another page, another story, Jackanory!

Though our role is specifically the protection of the paintings, we do more of one thing that was originally never part of the job descrip' and that is give directions.
It can be quite repetitive like a traffic light but the standpoint - get it? - is hardly hard, so getting paid for giving some helpful information seems incredibly reasonable. Yet it's still a chore for some while they are STILL sitting on their derrieres.
Now the flipside if you will, is how utterly rude and offensive some people of planet earth can be and I know it sometimes feels like 'I'm mad as hell, and I'm not going to

take this anymore' before you blow your brains out with your imaginary pistol.

We all deal with members of the ignoramus club differently but to save a lot of time and frustration, simply give them less time. With some, no time.

When I'm accosted by the 'hoi polloi' without a greeting or courtesy, even interrupted in some cases, my conduct switches as quick as a comb into a flick-knife. Without a single syllable from my lips I point in a broad direction which is closer to leaving my vicinity than to their loutish demands. Silence is not only golden but a glorious rebuff!

If only they showed a mediocre of manners, I could share so much with them; enlightenment, excitement, warmth and waggishness.

Sometimes I'm giving direction to someone and already they are walking before I finish. Cockamamie! It's a wonder they can wait to breath. You'll find me waving to the backs of the heads as they can 'get lost!'

And there is the visitor who has no clue – internal compass broken – and unable to understand simple directions. 'Hey, take my hand and I will bring you there. In fact I will push you around in a wheelchair and give you a fucking cup of 'cha' with a bloody toasted tea-cake to boot!'

The great unwashed that is the public nuisance can go jump into the fountains outside.

'Members,' the paying clientele and the oft quoted 'the customer is always right' poppycock. Consumer rights are kosher but when they wave their plastic like shiny, shiny badges, demanding this and that and speak to staff like serfs, well it only pisses us off. And when we can put them in their place with the rest of us, well it is a little victory. It is all we have.

Now phones. Regardless of the rules which can be a hindrance and a headache from Hades, I simplify it with a sprinkle of bon-sens. Unless they chatting like a demented Dom Jolly, I let it slide for a while. Maybe let them know I know and if after a while they still natter, I'll ask them only once to take it to another continent. And I will certainly not get into an argument over a fucking mobile like some of my fellow fanatics who pounce with such zealousness you'd think they were soldiers ready to die for their cause. It's just a phone for Allah's sake!

Rules are rules you say but I feel they are more a quagmire of guidelines or a quicksand of implications!

They are the 'Don Quixote's' of the National. Sponsored by 'Meryl Peril' and fantasizing drama in the humdrum. Filling mundane with mush. Power and purpose discombulated and the trip ends up undermined.

Fools and tools akin to a DIY disaster!

Spare parts are given radios. They think it's a license to meander, socialise or hideaway in the computer room. It goes to their head like fizzy-static. There are those who think they are doing you a favour but anyone can let me go eye-lash!

And there are those that do themselves no favour. Domineering and deranged they hold radios like sceptres and everyone eyes them sceptically. There's a streak of the irrational like jumping in the deep end before the pool's been filled.

There is a difference between being ready for trouble and expecting trouble. Like an invitation and an intrusion. That P.O.V. is counterproductive. Expect the worst and you will get what you always got!

Putting yourself forward is putting yourself up for gallows humour and if you like being a brown-nosing busy-body then learn to put up with the smell of bureaucratic bullshit!

And don't even think of using your initiative, that's almost illegal. Not part of your contract. Common sense should be left in your locker.

And I know it feels like duty is what no one else will do at the time but hey, join the club of 'Why Bother' where our motto is 'Oleum et operam pedis.' Loosely translated – 'There's little truck to give a fuck!'

'Why haven't you mentioned the 'white shirts?'' I hear someone ask. Team Leaders and Deputies for the uninitiated.

Yes indeed, they are as much vegetables in this soup and so are many in numerous departments but this is all about the frontline; the toy soldiers going back and forth in the rooms. The 'white shirts' themselves would have a dynastic book of their very own!

'Yeah! What do the Team Leaders and Deputies do anyway?'

Well if you don't understand, don't criticise. It was a derogatory remark underlined with disrespect. How easily they forget.

How can you blacken the white shirts yourself when all you do in the rooms is rehearse retirement. And if you're not fiddling with a phone or reading your newspaper clippings, filling out betting slips, then you're still attempting to finish a two-year old crossword or writing that book!

I haven't even touched upon the 'talking.' You must be on piece-work for every single grunt and groan that falls out of that 'ga-ga' mouth of yours.

Whether in jest, envy or mutton-headiness, they are quick to forget how they have been ministered by a 'care-worker' of sorts. All the favours and flavours they wanted were provided with a lifeline and they just kept on sucking. A piggish child on a mother's teats. And boy - or girl - they were mothered.

All the tantrums and tussles they broke up when rattles were thrown from prams. All the times you made a mess in your room and the Team Leaders, Deputies turned up to mop up your homemade shit. Even did your work for you, what little you manage to fuck up!

Anyway, enough of that before I am accused of taking the side of our 'frenemy.' So in answer to the above question 'What do the Team Leaders and Deputies actually do?' I say 'More than we bloody do. A lot more'

It reminds me of the joke – How many gallery assistants does it take to give directions? All of 'em because they have fuck else to do!'

Yo Crazy Cat Kath! It's you I'm looking at. You're a hyperactive absurdity and a frettin' too much. Look around ya, do you see anyone else who really gives a fig. You gotta let it go, it just ain't worth it girl. The sooner you embrace this, the less living daylights you'll lose.

The DJ in my jukebox head always plays Diana Ross's 'Do you know where you're going to?' whenever I see her. She jigs back and forth on eggshell heels and the squawk of a radio puts her on tenterhooks. But she sure is pretty. Reminds me of Vigee le Brun's self-portrait.

Crazy Cat Kath changed her mind as often as the seconds on the clock and like the hands always ended up back at odds with herself. I suppose decisiveness for her was something AWOL. It was like her mind had decided long ago that if it was up to her, it wouldn't be up to her.
Scatterbrain that she is, she once turned up for work on her day off.
''Do you know where you're going to?''

That is Joshua Reynolds' Anne, Second Countess of Albemarle. She roams the gallery like a Dicken's apparition and is just as old fashioned as lard. She seems to float around room to room in a silent wailing, her mouth incessantly agape like a child with Moebius Mouth and a face as ashen as rice paper. When she does speak it is whispered like a librarian with laryngitis.
There she was wafting around the Espresso Bar Bristol fashion collecting empty coffee cups like she was taking back empty lemonade bottles.
Akin to a ghostly cleaner she continued her haunting and I was never sure if she was moonlighting, volunteering or simply had nothing better to do?

'How dare they?'
'Eh?'
'Who do they think they are?'
'Who?'
'The sheer cheek of it.'
'What?'
Moody Judy! Wife of Govaert van Surpele, Catherina Coninckx

huffed and puffed her way over and told them 'I'm not having it.'

'Then we'll use it.' The rebuff came back hilariously.

'Their sitting on my chair.' She squealed in my direction. It looked like four school kids were attempting to break some world record by all trying to seat on it at once. 'They're gonna break it!'

'Do you think so?' one of the record breaking attempters said hopefully.

I found it all entertaining.

It happens and when the visitor parks their bottom on the novelty leather, they are eyed like ne'er'-do-well trespassers.

Is it the only representation of the – pardon the 'Ha!' – seat of power that you possess? Would it be a loss of authority and control to give it up occasionally? Or is it the undesirability of your innate program? The caveman had it and so does your next door neighbour; territorial pissings!

Don't get into an argument about it. It is only a chair. It is not a throne. And chair rhymes with share, so synonymous, so there!

Now all you're flapping, it don't amount to much and it certainly does not merit a disciplinary. There's a lack of common sense a lot of the times and some staff are unable to deal and diffuse the easy-peasiest of matters. They cry out for a team leader for every drop of spilt milk.

Many of us deal with situations little and large every day without brownie points. So stop wasting everybody's time and justify your wages for once.

That's Solly Benson. Nicknamed 'Sully' because it's the complete opposite of the man himself. Obviously.

He has OD-ed on OCD and walks like a Master Graduate from the Ministry of Silly Walks. Moving and swaying around objects and people like they carry a contagion. He is just as tall and lanky as John Cleese too and looks like that dork with the glasses in Bruegel's Adoration of the Kings.

He will not touch anything he does not have to which seems an almost impossibility in any walk of life. Hangs by doors like an ineffectual porter so he does not have to open it, slipping through as it closes like a contortionist. Not using his hands, his feet are utilised like a quadriplegic and the last resort is always the stretched ragged sleeve of his jumper that functions as a handkerchief.

Don't make the mistake of handing him the panic alarm – he will not take it. Leave it under the seat where everyone else seems to put it with the allotment of used chewing gum.

Sully has more hand soap and tissues on him than an A&E and it is a wonder his hands haven't diluted the amount of times he cleans them. And God man! The pervading stench of sanitizer - he's OD-ed on OCD reeking of TCP!

I spot a fellow inmate a few rooms away and stick my fingers up at him. He immediately guffaws back shaking the paintings on the wall and the curiosity of all. The public do not expect it; they perceive us as unspeaking monoliths or eyeballing busts.

Crunchie Chuck reminded me of the lion from the 'Wizard of Oz.' Cuddly, approachable - a pussy cat. His mane was the colour of a Crunchie bar's interior and he was not that dissimilar to Domenichino's lion in 'The Vision of Saint Jerome.'

I liked this guy and many people misunderstood him. He was an American but you can't blame him for where his geography born him.

Sure he was loud and talked a lot but he was interesting as any of the history in this place and was a walking, talking set of encyclopaedias. Who needed the Information Department when you had Crunchie Chuck? And he would actually listen to you which couldn't be said for the rest of the self-absorbed sponges in this place!

It was approaching 'shutting-up shop' and Boring Noreen had been promoted to toilet concierge. She had to stop by on her way like a vulture in the sky.

'It's getting worse.' She has been saying every day for the last twenty years. How worse can worse get, I always wondered?

They got a hundred and one reasons to be miserable about but they are not reasons. More a verbal extension of a fed-up sigh. Or the rattling exhaust of a clapped-out car!

If you give time and energy to these things then they will only gnaw. By feeding them you are allowing them to overrun like weeds in the mind.

She and her playfellow suspects represented my variety of the ole' proverb 'An allegory of Prudence.'

'Have they learned from yesterday?

When today they act lame.

By their very actions,

Tomorrow will be the same.'

Now you probably think all of this is somewhat 'a side of cynicism' but I'm only stripping off the uniforms here. I haven't even begun to scratch the surface, only the un-ironed scruffy edges. So don't be offended by the naked truth – we all defecate and everyone's neurotic to some degree of peculiarity. To be fair and bring some equilibrium to all of this, I think it is only right to talk about all the positive personalities that bring much joy to their roles as ambassadors to the grand ship that is the National.

It is akin to the United Nations here and all the colourful and cultured personalities as much part of the gallery as the paintings. They bring their worldly light to many visitors experience. As approachable, engaging and knowledgeable as even the babbling 'Robert Langdon' curators and the long-winded 'Dan Brown' lecturers.

It's the staff in rooms that can make the difference from an enjoyable visit for the visitors to an eclectic one. These 'exceptionals' I see not as guards but guardians. Pantheons in their enthusiasm and intelligence. National treasures themselves. Like old masters they have their value too.

As egregious as some can be sometimes - the mediocre and the miserable - there are a many diamonds in the rough that can sparkle your working day when all is dull elsewhere. Personalities that pick you up when you're pissed off. Cheer you up when you're feeling pickled. When peace of mind is better than giving them a piece of your mind.

Days when you go home with sore cheeks from smiling and laughing and you got paid for that too.

We peer down at the scuffs on our shoes with recollections reflected in each - scratches and scars that the playground inflicts and then, there she blows; the call to close and the working dead are reanimated. Stirred from slumber. Relief and ejaculation aerosol faces and limbs, as the melee depart.

Then the signal and akin to the end of school bell we run like inmates from the institution. Excitable shrieks akin to races to the dorms and the hubbub of the locker room an arcade. Unburdened banter as we get into civvies and make our escape.

Dragging our heels and scuffing our gallery issues. There's no place like our playground.

Afterword

All I'm doing is remarking upon the idiosyncrasies we all inadvertently portray in any given day. All the improper and compulsive conduct that I have witnessed. I'm no different. I've learnt my lessons a long time ago.

I started this before our nearest and dearest gallery was privatised. This is a representation of those civil servant days and still is in some ways. Some things haven't changed and neither have we – the still serving and loyal serfs.

I hope I have not offended but we cannot deny our true nature in the rooms. We are only neurotically human.

'Cum grano salis.'

January 2017

META – RAGE

'ATTENTION PLEASE. ATTENTION PLEASE. FIRE HAS BEEN REPORTED IN THE BUILDING. PLEASE EVACUATE THE BUILDING IMMEDIATELY....'
The broadcast clamoured like a self-service checkout.
'... STAFF WILL DIRECT YOU TO THE NEAREST EXIT.'
What staff there was the majority had already joined the exodus.
In blind panic the public ran every which way which only confused them even more. Some collided with each other like headless chickens and fought with flapping arms to get through the stampeding migration. Others fell to the floor and quickly scrabbled back up onto their feet only to run off in the completely opposite direction.
Between the announcements the electronic alarm 'bleeped' like a vehicle reversing. 'PLEASE EVACUATE THE BUILDING IMMEDIATELY....'

The screams and cries of people became so raucous that it almost drowned out the tannoy broadcast. It sounded like a playground at the start of playtime.

'… STAFF WILL DIRECT YOU TO THE NEAREST EXIT.'

There was not much assisting or directing. It was the classic reaction of the mob mentality; pandemonium manhandled the masses. Nevertheless a few canny visitors tailed some of the fleeing purple-shirted staff heading for the exits. Just like the White Van Man behind a hurrying ambulance, they kept up with the uniforms that would lead them to salvation and photo opportunities.

At the top of the main staircase two charitable members of the staff that had remained, lingered nonchalantly and herded the startled sheep down the steps. It was probably another false alarm, they assumed. Happened all the time.

'… Down the stairs now. No need to panic, take your time.' One of them urged with windmills arms.

'BLEEP…! BLEEP…! PLEASE EVACUATE THE BUILDING IMMEDIATELY….'

'What is it then?' The other asked.

'Dunno! An explosion of some sort, I heard.' He replied with a shrug of his shoulders. 'And a leak of something toxic, I heard too.' He sounded like he didn't even believe anything of what he said.

'… STAFF WILL DIRECT YOU TO THE NEAREST EXIT.'

'Down you go. Nice and easy.' The other boomed as another pocket of people came spilling out of the rooms. 'Not a fire then?'

'Not that I heard mate.'

Very rarely was it a threat. The announcement and drills were usually planned in advance in such a large and complex building. They concurred someone had probably burnt their toast again.

They stepped back a little, giving themselves some more space from the stampede. It resembled a Black Friday Sale! 'Think Eve's involved.' He rumoured.

'Again…?' the other tutted. 'Figures. Red and green should never be seen….'

They finished the ditty together. '…. She's best avoided the Red Queen.' Chuckling at each other like munchkins.

They watched as a plump woman slipped on the concrete staircase but luckily land on her somewhat large derriere. People ran past and even leapt over her without stopping and somehow avoided a pile-up of flustered flesh.

The ruffled woman eventually picked herself up and continued to move lopsided down the stairs rubbing her rotund rump.

'Lucky lump!' one of the guards stated then turning to deaf ears, he reiterated loudly to the horde. 'Take your time going down the stairs please.'

Both men observed the squeeze through the main doors with detachment. They could have been watching television so laid-back were they!

'BLEEP…! BLEEP…! PLEASE EVACUATE THE BUILDING IMMEDIATELY….'

A flustered red faced man rushed up to the two guards. Breathing heavily and legs crossed, he yelped in a foreign accent 'Toy-let! Toy-let!'

'… STAFF WILL DIRECT YOU TO THE NEAREST EXIT.'

'You gotta be kidding me amigo?' He looked to his colleague whose eyebrows seemed about to be join the scramble.

The other uttered under his breath 'People never cease to amaze…' and to get the message across yelled 'This is an emergency man. Get outta here!'

'Please, please, please….' The squirming visitor pleaded. His eyes squinted, holding something in.

'Please, please, please… Make. Your. Way. Out of the building, NOW!' The guard pressed home like he was spoon-feeding a cotton-eared geriatric.

With a whimper, the bursting red faced man turned with hands between his legs and hopped down the stairs.

'Unbeliev-a-bubble.' The guard galled.

'Never underestimate the stupidity of people.' The other stated with a shake of his head.

'BLEEP…! BLEEP…! PLEASE EVACUATE THE BUILDING IMMEDIATELY….'

'Down the stairs now people. No need to rush. London Town awaits your dosh.'

'… STAFF WILL DIRECT YOU TO THE NEAREST EXIT.'

But still the public masses hopped and skipped. Their shrieks continued unabated. Playtime wasn't over yet!

The two guards continued to assist in the evacuation until they spotted more and more of their own purple shirts amongst the fray. Was there anymore staff left in the building? They looked at each other with the same question and both their indifferent expressions answered each other.

Like escapees from the institution they joined the dash towards the exit too.

To this day I still couldn't comprehend that a cushy colleague at that could get so unexpectedly worked up and enraged in a job that was simply the easiest in the world.

So much so, to the point that she literally exploded! And believe me that is not far from the truth.

It was a one of a kind unsettling and freak occurrence that still shocked me and stumped all the scientific experts to this day. Certain aspects had faded in the memory and a little embellishment grew to the point that it had become a myth of sorts; a glorified tale that changed in each telling recall. A fantastical story it would become, to tell all and sundry about regardless of who was there to witness it or not and it is precisely this attitude and assumption of people that may well of caused this extraordinary affair in the first place. That inexplicably started Eve Green's descent into a horrifying and alienated rage.

It was much later after the inexplicable event when I discovered what it was that had set her off for the last and fatal time. An accumulation of episodes during that infamous date and on top of the months and months of anger and resentment building up, it finally came to a boiling point that she erupted.

As early as opening time she was heard arguing with a member of the public who had accused her of being rude – after all that had happened, I could well believe it and so another complaint form was filled out with her name on it. Human Resources should have given her, her very own supply of forms.

My bulging records showed it was her fifth complaint in eight months. Was she trying to get herself a gallery record and that did not include the many more that I stepped in, diffused and did not report. It was plain to see she was getting into more and more pickles and all of them for unnecessary reasons. For the life of me, I couldn't understand why she was making the job so difficult for herself. I always told my team, that there was no real need to get into confrontations because as long as you sat in the rooms and watched the public, the job did itself. Many of my team encountered these same instances she did every day and handled themselves calmly and professionally. Why couldn't she? She seemed to set out and go looking for trouble.

Then at lunchtime down in the staff quarters, she was heard vociferously complaining about the weekend rota that had been posted up and how she had been assigned loathsome duties yet again – to her, all duties were loathsome, even the most undemanding. Anybody who had not even seen but heard the hollering knew only too well who it was. The Red Queen had lost it again! Doors were slammed and bins kicked and it didn't matter who got in the way because she could see nothing else but - pardon the pun - red.

'Eve you have to get on with it whether you like it or not.' I told her once. 'Everybody else does.' But alas, to her there was no disambiguation.

She was fuming like a stirring volcano and with the trivial events of earlier and all that had gone before building up, she had returned to her room and eventually blew!

The establishment had been emptied of all public and only a dozen members of the senior staff remained. A skeleton crew oversaw the continuing crisis; answering calls, monitoring cameras and checking no one else was meandering the premises when they shouldn't be. Unaffected points in the gallery were locked down with fire, flood and blast doors. As the emergency services arrived and were let in, the back gates were immediately sealed closed.

At the front of the building Rita Price - one of the remaining senior members of the staff was waiting at the main doors to meet and escort her three high-level guests. She was short and eighteen stone of prim and proper and her uniform was immaculate on her round body. Her bleached dyed blond hair was tied up in a severe bun and a lot of make-up plastered her tanned Oompa-Loompa face. She paced back and forth like the balls of Newton's Cradle and continually checked the time on her mobile.

She still couldn't quite digest what had happened. When she had finally made it into the room after bullishly pushing her way through the fleeing crowds running against her, she found the most unexpected thing she had ever seen in her whole life. What looked like a gargantuan pink marshmallow!

To her utter disbelief she was then informed by a colleague that the 'thing' was her team member, Eve Green!

She thought he was having a laugh and she did laugh, cackling like a Tommy gun. Surely it was a joke. Another one of her colleague's wind-ups that they were prone to do and Eve had actually fled the building with the rest of the staff.

Back in the lobby Rita's ruminations were interrupted by the arrival of the three specialists - two men and a lamppost of a woman. Rita had to stop ill-treating her upturned neck and close her uncorked mouth.

The lady wore black pleated trousers and a buttoned up jacket to match. She towered over the men like an Alberto Giacometti sculpture and made Rita feel like a garden gnome. The men wore suits, one smart and pressed, and the other slept-in, creased. The 'chic' one was good looking and had a Hollywood quality about him that she found immediately stirring. The other man was not so interesting, an atypical professor type with a soup strainer moustache.

'Hello.' Rita began loud and proud. She was gregarious and engaging with everyone she met and spoke with a 'pie and mash' accent. 'I'm Rita Price, here to escort you and answer any of your questions. I'm also the team leader to my colleague that has supposedly…' she exaggerated the word with exaggeration. '…been the cause of all of this.'

They could tell that she didn't believe any of it.

The two men let the tall lady introduce herself first, 'Doctor Ida Scorel.' She said with a caramel European cadence.

Rita noticed she was not skinny but broad and lean in a mannish way and despite the awkwardness of her physique, she allured. She reminded Rita of the actress Sigourney Weaver but with long blond hair tumbling down past her flat behind.

The mopped grey haired dishevelled man of medium height and slight stoop had a dead fish hand shake. He wore small round specs on a porridge face and in a tepid voice, he introduced himself as simply Professor Morales.

Then stepped forward 'Doctor Marinus van Aertsen, a pleasure.' He said in a silky tone and charming manner. His hand was warm and Rita was already missing it. He was the antithesis of what a doctor or professor should be and his accent was American chat-show host.

The meet and greet was abruptly interrupted by another group of men from the Fire Brigade clobbering past them, clattering and clinking in their uniforms, helmets and equipment. It was a wonder they could move at all, Rita simpered at the sight of men in uniform. Maybe they should lose an item or most!

'Lead the way, please Rita.' Dr. van Aertsen snapped her out of it. 'As I'm sure you know, time is an important factor here.'

'Yes of course.' Rita smouldered back from one daydream to another.

Putting an arm around her that did not actually touch - he had to be careful not to pick up another lawsuit - he implored 'Along the way, perhaps you can give us a brief profile of your colleague involved?'

Touch me if you want handsome. 'Certainly.' Rita answered and with a flick of her tail, spun around and hopped off like a hopping bird.

Her fleetness took them by surprise and kick-started themselves through the empty rooms and halls after her. Their footfalls echoed like the tapping of Morse Codes as they hurried to keep up with Rita whose heels each time struck the wooden floorboards clamorously like the galloping hooves of Lady Godiva's horse.

Since it happened he hadn't stopped laughing. His cheeks and jaw hurt and occasionally his body convulsed in a fit which stitched his side. He could not remember the last time he laughed so hard.

'The wicked witch is dead!'

Though he was in front of a television screen, he wasn't watching the 'Wizard of Oz.' It was one of the six CCTV monitors in the control room where he worked and he had replayed the same footage over twenty times now and each time he found it more hilarious.

'Ding dong the witch is dead. The wicked bitch is dead.' Ludolf Gate guffawed aloud. He didn't think there was anything wrong with speaking to himself. Didn't everybody?

The seclusion of the building and the late hours suited him. The less he had to do with people, the better and yet ironically, he watched people all the time.

He was a South African, large and lazy and told people 'Take me how you want.' He didn't give a shit about anybody.

And most people didn't give a shit about him!

Albeit a little late, he had finally hit the fire alarm. Through the garbled and quacking overlapping radio calls and panic alarms, he had sussed that something was going down. All he could do now was wait for the evacuation of all public and non-essential staff and as he watched the 'Keystone Cops' scenes play out on his screens, he picked his nose and ate what he found up there.

'Never liked her.' He told himself like it was the first time.

'Oh really Ludolf. Pray tell…' he spoke in a hoity-toity female voice.

'She's a rude bitch.' He illustriously declared in his Afrikaans' accent.

In his mind he rerun each and every incident and encounter with her like the recordings on his monitors. Her refusal to ever acknowledge his 'good mornings' or 'hello's,' never holding a door open and leaving it to shut in his face. She was as polite as a dingo!

She was also incapable of doing her duties at all when she was assigned deputising or patrolling – was about as useful as a 'Muggie!' I mean what was the radio for? A fucking accessory! And when she did use it, no one understood a bloody word she was saying. It was like listening to a 'dronkie.' She may as well have shoved it up her arse!

He reached inside his shirt pocket and pulled out some warm M & M's and pushed them into his mouth.

She was a pain in the arse to a lot of people; it wasn't just him. He heard it and saw it on the monitor's every day. She looked for trouble and that was fucked-up troubling. Many a time he observed her bulldozing and mauling of visitors and staff. It was like a comedy of errors, a hilarious tragedy of ineptitude and he could not get enough of her dingbat shit. Once before, she even pushed the fire alarm, convinced she saw smoke coming out a dustbin in the staff corridor. She hadn't and the more she was questioned about it, the more she became doubtful of herself; embarrassed and angry at the whole situation. It didn't help that colleagues would jibe her by yelling 'Fire!' every time they saw her. It was one of the reasons why when the alarm went off in her room, no one initially took it seriously. Himself included.

Staff rolled their eyes at each other and wondered what it was now, that she was crying over. Every time she had pushed her panic button, it had been found out to be only spilt milk.

It wasn't amiss to him that watching her on the CCTV was very much like watching reality TV. Even downstairs in the staff area when their breaks coincided, he would see her tagging along with a few of her minions and the excitement and enthusiasm so put on. Trying to show her enemies that there was nothing wrong with her, that she was absolutely fabulous and you were missing out by not loving her. A false bonhomie and it was so pretentious that she couldn't see how fake she came across. She was prima donna without the prima and without a doubt, no Madonna!

She was mad. All you had to do was look at that candy floss hair. I mean who in their right mind would dye their barnet the colour of a Baboon's arse? Her needle was broken and her record scratched. She was cuckoo!

He liked that. 'She's cuckoo! Cuckoo! CUCKOO!

He clucked at a freeze-framed image of her in the room.

'Dead cuckoo!' he honked.

Pulling himself out of his sticky chair, he stood up and began to prance around the control room imitating a chicken. 'Cluck, cluck, cluck, cluck, cluck!'

'That's her. Cluck! Cluck!' He belly-ached. Then a thought struck him. She had reminded him of an animal and he couldn't quite place it and it began to bug him. He stopped being the 'bird' and sat back at his console.

Googling, he finally found an image of a pink-faced Bald Uakari monkey.

He roared at his apt discovery. 'Yep! Yep, that's her.'

His jaw and his sides continued to ache.

At first, Rita didn't believe any of it. Thought it was just the usual gossip and rumours that did its rounds in the gallery. Nevertheless what was being said and heard more and more frequently was about Eve and subsequently more people were at the battering end of her escalating tantrums. As her personal demons fed on a junkie's diet of cynicism and jealousy, more and more complaints were being made against her. A pattern was forming like skid marks! Was what people saying about her actually true? Rita had to find out for herself and tactfully began to observe her.

Eve approached everybody and every situation antagonistically. You saw the tell-tale signs as her Dianthus hair stood on end like a spooked cartoon cat. Her glorified guard straddled for something that needed no confrontation yet she found drama in stale. Every visitor that came through the doors only wanted to tick a box on their tourist's trip, not actually have a boxing match!

Every trifling thing was a peccadillo to her character. Public at a leeway distance from a painting was considered too close and akin to crossing the De-militarized Zone. If anyone erroneously questioned her it was an affront to her authority, an insult and if a rule was breached or broken, it was an act of war. She could no longer politely point out guidelines; her pointing finger has become a pistol. It was as if she had declared war on every human being. Some demented vendetta that she could only understand.

One day with the public present and tickled by this unexpected spectacle by supposedly professional security staff, there was a full blown argument in the gallery rooms between Eve and another team member - Cee. I later discovered it had something to do with time-keeping, over a pitiful five minutes and it was a colleague who was known for good punctuality. Cee had tried to explain the delay but Eve refused to listen, only accused and insulted. So Cee did what many had wanted to do for a long time. She stood up to her and told her to her face that she was intolerable, egoistical and poison. Worthy of the nickname doing the rounds.

'What was that?' Eve screamed back. Of course, in her insecurities she had to know. Had to step into the hole!

'Red Queen! You're the Red Queen.' Cee was glad she had got it off her chest. Brave enough to have a go at Eve when everyone else was afraid to.

'That's what everyone's calling you. The Red Queen! Ha! Ha!' Cee finished with a gleeful flourish.

Taken aback and unable to return any vocal venom, Eve fled the room in a rage with her thunder face and beacon hair. Colleagues especially enjoyed the show; got a kick out of the Red Queen's own self-made pickle!

Cee was the gallery heroine and colleagues forever after 'high-fived' her for being so candid.

The nickname was based on the 'Alice in Wonderland' character but the more recent 'Helen Bonham-Carter' movie incarnation. Apt it was too, as it was a play on her ridiculous hair dyes that she tortured her hair with. It wasn't even red but an awful pink Day-Glo. On the face of it - or the head - her original hair colour seemed to have a pig-headed mind of its own and had spurned and rejected the dye. As if it would not accept this foreign invasion or the fakery of it and as stubborn as its owner, the hair reacted oppositely. In its refusal to take the colour, all the dye could do was fabricate something close to red and it failed catastrophically.

'Red and green should never be seen. She's best avoided, the Red Queen!'

Rita had occasionally overheard that ditty doing the rounds and sung with a similar rhythm to the 'Teddy Bears Picnic.' She found it quite amusing and found herself humming it whenever Eve came up. Who started it, no-one knew or admitted and so catchy and ingrained it became despite its silliness, she began to realise she had no control over it. Something in her brain put the record on and she had to bite her tongue in fear of blurting it out aloud. 'Red and green should never be seen. She's best avoided, the Red Queen!'

Rita had observed enough. Something was bothering Eve – that was plain to see. She was almost a different person, unrecognisable and a little bit intimidating to be honest. Most people were avoiding her like a pissed-off crocodile.

She began to enquire in confidence to trustworthy members of staff. How they found her of late?

'Moody and pathetic.' Someone growled.

A first aider simply said 'Self-inflicted. Has only herself to blame.'

'Distance.' The closest person she had to a friend replied down in the mouth.

'As miserable as Macbeth.' Ludolf scoffed with a mouthful of pepperoni.

Leslie the Les who fancied her, shed tears.

'Don't get me started…' A deputy started. 'That woman is both tyrannical and a child.'

The resident Plato said, 'The person that does not like themselves will not like you. The colour of their soul is black and blue!'

'A downright pain in the ar…' Rita had heard enough.

Eve hadn't helped herself by shutting most people out. Excluded herself from most of her colleagues who eventually had less time for her. People simply did not what to be in her crash wreck company.

Was this a breakdown that we were witnessing, Rita mused. Or were we on the receiving end of the vindictive games envious people play? Whatever it was, Rita realised she had an onion to peel!

They grouped around the console, bending over and peering at the screen which showed a gallery room in a tincture image. The control room was piddling as it was and now with Rita and the three boffins it felt like a closet. They had very little room to move and just about avoided stepping onto each other's toes. Dr. Scorel stooped to avoid dusting down the ceiling and when she leaned over, she loomed over everybody like an inquisitive giraffe.

Ludolf jiggled with the remote control joystick that zoomed in and out of the screen as it played out the CCTV footage, speeding it up to only moments before the event.

He was an elephantine man in a stretched to splitting uniform of a never ironed white shirt and food stained trousers. There was also a nose turning odour of B.O. orbiting him.

'Keep an eye on that b…..' He stopped himself in time but it was too late. All present had got the nub. He rubbed his sweaty forehead uneasily with his yellowed sleeve.

Rita shook her head displeased. The man had no professionalism or decorum.

It was common knowledge, the man's disdain of Eve and often Rita and others heard his verbalisation of the Red Queen. Yet he never had anything else to talk about? As much as you tried to chat about anything else, he always brought her up and often he was caught scrutinising her on the CCTV footage whenever anybody visited the control room. Hunched over it like some slobbering omnipresent Quasimodo. Anybody with an aversion to her and spend so much time was bordering on the obsessive. It was an unhealthy fascination. Rita often entertained whether he was in denial and actually fancied her. A kind of aversion attraction of lust and hate.

Ludolf continued. '….on the woman, the guard sitting on the chair.' A fat greasy finger pointed and smeared the monitor.

They leaned in closer much to their nostril's protestations. On the monitor half a dozen members of the public could be seen moving in and out of the doorways, ambling around the mausoleum like room while perusing the paintings on the walls. The guard was perched unladylike on the room's chair. One leg up and crossed over the other – if she wasn't wearing trousers the colour of her knickers would be waving – and an arm idled over the back of the chair, resting behind her head. Unflattering, she had the appearance of a Madam in a brothel.

Rita always thought Eve resembled a staunch pigeon with twig like legs that were contradictory to the rest of her body and her bricklayer's shoulders. Crayon crimson hair hung off her small head like mutant ivy. Her nose and lips were charitable but her pale complexion made her appear washed out. On a good day her eyes were an appealing green but once rage set in they turned into pond algae. If only she scowled less and smiled more like she used to, she was quite pretty.

What happened to her, Rita pondered? What was the real root that had turned her once positive outlook to mud? What was the undeniable and underlining cause that changed her character so drastically? She had turned from Jekyll into Hyde and Hyde was staying!

The quality of the monitor's image was astonishing. Revealing even the smallest details like the subconscious tick where Eve persistently picked at a hair under her chin that never seemed to get plucked. Maybe it actually wasn't there? Rita inferred much like her will-o'-the-wisp paranoia. She could even be seen chewing her gum - never without one - her anxieties fuelling it with the perpetual pistons of her lantern jaw jerking up and down!

Then suddenly, a blink of the eye and part of the image exploded akin to a deteriorated film stock burning and bubbling. Rapidly this smear started to expand and grow and before long, began to fill the room and the camera view.

'Fascinating.' Scorel uttered as she towered over them all even closer to the screen.

Van Aertsen stroked his chin to a point and Morales frowned at it incredulous.

Ludolf must have watched this footage again and again like a YouTube video but still uttered 'Bladdy insane!' He licked his lips and sleeved his brow, sweating like a microwaved sausage roll.

He was asked to replay it again which he did five more times while the scientists continually scrutinised it silently behind him. Rita could almost hear their thought processes trying to form diagnosis.

Van Aertsen's silky tones requested Ludolf zoom in at the far end of the room where backed up against the wall two members of the public had become trapped. The doorways were now blocked off by the ever increasing mass. Two victims, one – a woman crouched down and curled herself into the foetal position, hands over her head like a petrified child. The man impossibly tried crawling his way up the wall behind him but left scarlet marks in the wallpaper where he tore his nails from his fingers. Silent screams mouthed until the mound of formless protoplasm finally consumed them, filled the room and the screen.

They all remained silent for a long time afterwards as this macabre image remained freeze framed on the monitor and their psyche forever.

The silence was palpable. All was heard was the trickle of the air conditioning unit until Ludolf scratched his crotch and cackled, 'There she blows!'

The gunfire racket from their weapons was deafening before it was cut short by the yelling and frantic sawing of hands in the air by the Fire Chief.

On hand too in this growing emergency the British Army had been called and into the building they had stormed like red ants and on encountering the enemy entity they had opened fire under the orders of their little Napoleon.

Trigger happy and at last able to see some action the squaddies went for it gung-ho, unleashing all their pent-up zeal into the pink ooze. Something in their years of training believed that shooting first would eradicate the problem yet the brief exercise of firepower had no effect whatsoever. They may as well as been using spuds guns. Their bullets disappeared into the thick sludge like peanuts into melting chocolate.

By now it had consumed and filled all of the North Wing and still it looked like some kind of toxic spillage albeit a fantastical percolating kind. There was an unreality to it – a Manga cartoon superimposed upon reality like a CGI special effect. It crawled at a snail's pace but because of its magnanimous mass appeared to move more consummately. Its growing volume engulfing everything in its path and filling every space, nook and cranny. As it ominously crept, it made a muted bubble wrap sound, randomly popping like cooking popcorn and as it consumed every fixture, furnishings, paintings and all objects in its way. It emitted a wet puckering sound liken to the licking of lips and satisfied fulfilment.

The Education Centre at the rear of the gallery was nearly swallowed up and it wouldn't be long before the 'stuff' pulverized its way out of the building and onto the street. Doors and shutters that had initially been closed and sealed, rooms and corridors locked down as in a fire drill made no difference as its sheer bulk and strength pushed aside and broke through these barriers like they were made of cardboard. Nothing could stop it. How long would it continue for? Would it begin to spill out of the building and into the neighbouring areas and ultimately consume the city like an apocalyptic blancmange!

All though the 'blob' - as it was now being called - had spilled off into adjacent hallways and rooms and other members of the fire crew and army surveyed these areas too, the main bulk or head of it was concentrated at this point in one of the larger rooms where a group of assorted mortals had congregated. They all observed it with a mixture of wonderment and fear as it slow-motioned poured in like strawberry custard. Some even took photos on their phones and sent texts. It seemed the vogue thing to do heedless of the danger.

The Fire Brigade and a troop of soldiers from the British Army maintained a safe distance while keenly observing it in case of any sudden changes or risks that could potentially arise. At the moment it was not a severe threat to people who could easily be evacuated in time but they had to be prepared for any deviation from its present threat. The main concern was its initial unpredictability and whether something as inexplicable like this could occur again. Not knowing what it was and how it would behave only emphasised the risk. The danger was always present albeit in slow motion.

Inchmeal the soldiers backed-up as the 'blob' encroached. Continually looking over their shoulders and making sure the civilians retreated further back closer to the nearest exit. They would have preferred these so called VIP's had 'fucked off' out of the building but they were members of the management and security teams and there for any questions the emergency services needed answering.

The yellow of the Fire Brigade and the green of the Army were separated into their own idiosyncratic groups. Each taking different sides of the room and it was representative of the divide and disagreement on both sides by the quarrelling of their respective leaders in the centre of the room. It was a stand-off between two stubborn contenders in the ring, in this arena of art.

'What in tarnation are you doing man?' The Fire Chief was furious and it didn't help that his eyes and ears were still blinded and ringing from the Army's earlier bombardment. 'This isn't a bloody battlefield.'

The Army Captain was short and squat like a Tolkien dwarf. Grey hair peeked out from under his beret that matched his grey toothbrush moustache. A boil that resembled Negitoro Sushi had taken up residence next to his nose.

He wasn't used to being shouted at. It was usually him doing the shouting. 'Trying to stop that.., that…' He didn't know what to call it. 'That thing…' he called it.

'That thing…' the Fire Chief turned his nose up at the moniker. '…. Is a unknown quantity and unknown quantities frighten me? Do you know how dangerous it is with your 'Rambo's' tearing all leather out of it with your blasted weapons? You could blow us and this place to kingdom come!'

The Fire Chief was shaven bald under his helmet and whatever moisturiser he used for his head appeared to cover his face too, giving him a glistening look of a roasting chicken.

The severity of the Fire Chief's words seemed to be lost on the Captain. 'My men are not 'Rambo's.'

'No. You're right. It's fucking Dad's Army here.'

'Now that's not nice.' Was all he could say and felt he was not in control of this situation at all? 'We are only attempting to control the situation.'

'There's no time for niceties Captain and I want no more of your shoot first and ask questions later. In case you haven't noticed that is not your typical enemy.' He took off his fire helmet and wiped his brow. Was it getting hot in here or was Captain Mainwaring getting on his tit?

'That 'thing'…' he again mocked. '…is not an invading army or a terrorist that you can halt with your pea-shooters. It is an unknown. Exposure, hazard and a possible 'Hazmat' need to be accountable for. Prevention may not be enough. Without knowing what we are dealing with, we may need an 'IAP,' possibly an 'IMT.'

The acronyms were lost on everyone present but the firemen.

The Captain's blood was beginning to boil like the boil living next to his nose. He was getting vexed with 'Barney McGrew.' Ha! He could call him names too, if not to his face. Feeling braver, he moved in closer.

'Now listen here.' His beret below the Fire Chief's chin. He tried to appear taller. 'I don't like your behaviour.'

'And I don't like your aftershave.' The Fire Chief spoke down to him literally. 'Back off.'

The captain backed off.

'Do you think you are helping here Captain?' His tone appeased but his annoyance didn't.

The Captain began to think he didn't and behind him, his men grinned at their superior's taste of his own medicine for a change.

'We're the experts here when dealing with substances and toxins of this nature. This is our job. We need to monitor and assess the situation. Find out what it is made of and what it is capable of doing? Take into account all the risk factors. How and if we can neutralise this threat or contain it?' He took a deep breath and wiped his sweaty brow again. Does this building know air-conditioning exists?

He continued, 'I have never come across anything like this before and in the short time we have, we need to

understand its nature. Every minute is precious.' He pacified. 'Do you want to help Captain?'
There was the coquettish of a nod from him.
'We are going to do this together. We can't be bickering here. People and this building are depending on us. We must be professional. And you Captain, you and your men are going to help by getting the fuck out of my way.'

They hurried from the control room, following the Team Leader Rita through the empty gallery rooms. If it wasn't for the urgency, it could have felt like a very private albeit whirlwind tour of this grand establishment.
As they scurried past the works of art adorning the walls, it soon became a blurred wallpaper of vain and uninterested faces and kaleidoscope landscapes.
The building evacuated of all the public felt jilted and it was a rare day that the National Gallery was closed during daylight hours. The majority of the staff was being urged to leave non-essentials posts. The few that remained scurried passed them in all directions, shouting on radios and mobiles phones, asking questions that no one knew the answers to.
Van Aertsen athletically ran to catch up with Rita, keeping in step with her pronounced power-walk. At least if they did lose sight of her around the many rooms and corners they passed through, they could follow the sound of her heels click-clopping like coconut shells.
Smiling the deliberate charm, he asked Rita 'Why the evacuation's delay?' It was a question that had been bugging him since they had arrived. 'Why did the staff not respond promptly?'
Rita dimpled back, eyes dreamy and continued the 'catch me if you can' pace. 'It happened so suddenly that initially

no one knew what was going on. In some cases the panic buttons did not work. The call wasn't made because the signal was not received.'

'Surely someone must have known? What about the building's detection devices?'

'That was the misunderstanding. Human and machine! No fire meant no danger or anything else for that matter.'

'That seems lax.'

'The whole place is complacent. Nothing ever happens here.'

She sharply turned a corner and Van Aertsen kept up like a faithful pup. The others were falling behind.

He could understand the complacency, inertia. When something has been the same for so long and nothing ever changes then reactions are wanton to be lackadaisical. If there's nothing to offset the urgency, there's no emergency. The radio calls that did come were a little too late, garbled and overlapping and once panic began it was difficult for staff to locate the source. People were fleeing in every direction, not knowing where to go or how to exit the building. Most of the staff on duty in the rooms fled too for their own safety, not giving a fig for public safeguards. Pandemonium run riot!

'A mob mentality! When confronted with fear, all duty and considerations went out the door. Just like they did themselves.' Van Aertsen surmised. 'It was a rational reaction. Unable to decide and see clearly, they followed the herd.'

'Obviously.' Rita wriggled her nose.

Before he could say another word, they had arrived in one of the larger and more impressive rooms of the gallery and Rita was astonished at how fast this thing was spreading. After all that had happened, it was beginning to sink in how alarming it was. It had already plugged the entire doorway from which it had come. Oozing into every expanse like the building was but a giant mould. It was like someone had placed a giant foam making machine, switched it on and let it fill the spaces. It was an enormous putty of fleshiness and made a soft crackling sound, peculiarly moreish to the ear and periodically, it expelled pockets of air like the breaking of wind.

It's the colour of her hair, Rita gasped at the actualisation. Was this a glimpse of the real Eve?

It would not be long before it spread to the next available exit. Mushrooming and seeking out every aperture; an unceasing viscous flow and unstoppable like the sea.

A platoon of soldiers marked their territories with spit and sweat. Hands on assault rifles they eyed the moving mass like watching molasses. Their Captain paced around the room like a spinning top.

The Fire Brigade ambled to one side with nothing to do. Like lemons holding leeks; their equipment was unused. They discussed how best to neutralise and contain this menace that they had no experience of whatsoever. It was literally a foreign body.

At a safe distance in the far end of the room by another exit, half a dozen suits were talking animatedly amongst themselves and gesturing towards the 'blob.' They were the Director of the National Gallery, a Trustee and two members of the security management. All that was missing were glasses of wine and some canapés and it would seem like a function was taking place so formal were they.

The three specialists stared at it in orgasmic fascination as it continued to almost silently creep into the room. It did not seem to frighten them, Rita noticed. If anything they gaped at it like a children in a chocolate factory. She supposed it was a wet dream for them!

On cue Dr. Scorel stated, 'It's gorgeous. Has an almost edible texture to it.'

Despite the oddity of the comment, Rita could see what Sigourney Weaver meant. It also reminded her of the 'Hubba Bubba' bubble gum she used to chomp as a kid.

The collective reverie was rudely interrupted by the bark of the Captain. 'MOVE BACK.'

His soldiers wanted to tell him that they had continually been 'moving back' but they remained tight-lipped and moved back some more. He had a need to shout, to be heard after his hosing by the Fire Chief. It was simply a case of authority for authority's sake.

Rita didn't know what to call that 'thing' now? Was there still some of Eve in that mess? Or was it as it looked, just a 'blob' without any residue of the human it once was? Either way, it was getting larger and larger and more and more fearsome.

Trying to understand why Eve should be behaving like this, I had called her into my office a few days before the infamous day and I still reflected whether that meeting had also escalated her breakdown or blow-up! But I wasn't going to feel guilty for that. I had tried, God I had tried!

I had a team to keep together and morale up. This was important to me despite some days it was like dealing with a troop of monkeys! As much as I advised and helped they exasperated me. But I could never show that. I had to remain proficient.

In my head, the ditty 'Red and Green' began to razzmatazz. I tried to ignore it.

'Hello Eve. Sit down darling.' Her green eyes flared like kangaroos in headlights and she appeared as weary as Saint Hubert exhumed. She was slumped on the chair her usual un-lady like way and despite my disapproval I let her continue chewing her cud like gum.

'I'm concerned about you Eve. I've received numerous and unfavourable reports about your working conduct from the public and colleagues alike.'

Her shoulders dropped away and she faux-sighed like a teenager.

'I've never had any complaints about you Eve and I always thought of you as a good worker and a valuable member of my team but lately you seem troubled. What is it Eve?'

Her mouth stopped gyrating and I thought she was going to say something but she stared vacantly at the plant pot on my windowsill.

With an attempt at amateur counselling, I continued. 'Would you like to talk to me hon' or someone else about it in confidence? We have members of staff for that sort of thing.'

She blushed to the roots of her hair, giving her the appearance of a salmon balloon. Changed her crossed leg to the other with a uncomfortable squeal from the chair and began to pick at that invisible hair under her chin. I thought that would annoy me too but I managed to remain sedated.

'You've always come to me before darling. Is there a problem at work or at home?

She spat it out so suddenly that I was almost ejected out of my chair. 'People, crowds, they're doing my head in. It's stressing me out.'

Then you're in the wrong job girl, I felt like telling her but as her Team Leader, I reminded myself I had to keep it professional. 'What can I or the gallery do to help?' I offered professionally. 'Would you like to go and have a chat with Occupational Health? See a councillor in confidence?'

She withdrew like a vampire in sunlight. 'No, No!' she shook her pink bonce. 'There's enough people talking about me already.'

And there and then, I understood the root of the grey matter. She stone-blind believed people were talking ill of her and in her unshakeable mind that was the problem because most people weren't. It was her homemade delusion blended up in a recipe of insecurities and jealousies and baked in a deeply underlying base of bitterness.

Albeit people naturally talked about her – people gossiped about people, that's what we do especially at work but she didn't help herself by being the talk of the town with all her nutty episodes. We were witnessing someone falling apart disastrously, drowning in her own soupcon!

Her colleagues took a certain kind of glee in what she had only brought upon herself. For some it was the highlight of the day to hear that she had gotten into another fine mess. Such distractions they came to expect and it made their humdrum hours less mundane. As long as they weren't on the receiving end, it was entertainment that got them around the clock.

It was clearly some kind of mental issue but whether that was to blame for all of it, I doubted it. The things she had said and done were not very nice and I didn't believe for a second that Eve had no control over her actions. You can't help how you feel but you can avoid what you are doing!

To some degree, she must have known what she was doing and she couldn't hide behind excuses. It all couldn't be blamed on stress or a malady. Something underlying was making her very unhappy and it may well be she didn't suit the job anymore. Maybe she had run its course. Room after room, day after day and was unable to stop going in circles and head-butting the same old walls and people. She may have felt the job was shit but you either rise above it or move on. Simple as that. Didn't someone once say; that if you find yourself in the same situations time after time then maybe your making terrible decisions. They are bad ideas and you need to change them.

Rita regarded herself something of a psychologist. Purely amateur of course but it had served her well. She had a keen interest in the topic and was more knowledgeable about the subject then most people realised. She knew it was this experience and education that made her get on with people. She learned to read body language and behaviour. Signs to look for and signs to avoid and she used it to her advantage. A life skill that helped her to get along with people and make day to day manageable for them and herself. She saw an idiosyncrasy to Eve's character that believed all the gossip as gospel but as soon as you told her about some stroke of luck or of something fortunate, she doubted it. Her calamity thrived on the negative that no matter how bad things were, they would always be worse. Rita only too well understood this affliction that was quite prevalent in a lot of people. Maybe this pessimism was making Eve wretched, a manifestation of her inadequacies and insecurities. Was it the common case of some people being unable to be pleased for others and had to make them as miserable as themselves? Hardened and worn thin cynical and distrustful of any trust itself!

It was getting tedious now. I couldn't help her no more and she certainly wasn't helping herself. I now saw a personality in whom something essential was missing. A person who fundamentally lacked that element of 'Will' which allows a human being to take hold and direct their own life.

Eve then mumbled, 'Maybe I need to get out of this place.' But I could see it was said without conviction.

Do us all a favour and go. Take your gum and ludicrous hair and don't come back no more, no more! We will miss you and your tantrums but I'm sure we will find something else to occupy our day with.

'Think about it Eve.' I resumed standard practise. 'Get some advice from family and friends before making a rash decision.' Adding to myself; because you sure have made plenty of those!

'I don't know.' She looked at the invisible hair in her finger that she thought she had picked and realising she hadn't, resumed tugging at her chin again.

'Maybe I'll have some time off, to think about it.' She coyly glanced at me in the expectancy that the eye contact would make everything hunky-dory.

She had had so much time off, she was practically retired. She had come up with so many excuses humanely possible for Human Resources that she would soon have to have a sex-change. She was called over more often than a prostitute on a street corner. All her annual leaves had been used up like scratch-cards and the book on her must have felled a rain forest.

Ignoring all this petty pleading, I remembered 'Now Eve, there is something else we have to address....' She suddenly looked condemned.

'... Human Resources have informed me that if they receive any more complaints from public and staff alike, you will have to attend a final disciplinary. Personally I have held them off for as long as I could and there have been many incidents which I have not reported to them. Now try and help me here to help you because I have done all I can without any legitimate explanations from you. I've bent over backwards for you and I will not any more. Sorry Eve.' I added subtly. There was no more 'hon,' 'darling' or sympathy.

She then snapped. Remonstrating to me that we were all ignorant because we did not understand her and we were all to blame. Apparently I, her colleagues and the world owed her something and we were all incredibly insensitive and selfish!

She then began to blurb. As her press-gang tears left tracks on her pale face, she rubbed her eyes again and again until her mascara had painted her face into a demented clown.

Before I could attempt at reassuring her, she ran out of the office shrieking like the melting Wicked Witch of the West!

A part of me was relieved. Disappointed at the outcome but bloody-hell relieved!

The Fire Brigade had tried everything in the book to neutralise the situation. All the 'Sizing-up,' 'Safe-Zoning' and even 'Pypolysis' – all standard procedures in fire-fighting had been utterly fruitless. The Chief's under garments were saturated and the sweat pouring from his manicured head stung his eyes like nitric acid.

The Army Captain and his troops could only watch as they continued to retreat. He felt a let down to the uniform and the bad dream he was living was 'Dunkirk' all over again for the British Army but in an art gallery!

Expectations were now on the scientists and they were not sure themselves. It was all theoretical but boy were they enjoying themselves. They had the look of geeks at a Star Wars convention and passed comments and prognoses back and forth to each other like thrilled teenagers.

One of the wooden suits from the other side of the room came clobbering over to where the scientists stood, the others followed like simulacra's.

Lanky with an ill-fitting three piece that hung off him like a curtain, he had the pallor of a worn out tea-towel. His black hair flopped in front of his elongated face and he continually flipped it back.

Brusquely, he introduced himself. 'My name is George Leighton, Director of the National Gallery. What are you doing to put an end to this dire situation?

He scowled at the Captain who glanced at the Fire Chief who looked at the scientists while Rita observed it all like a metaphorical game of 'pass the parcel.'

The scientists all eyed this scarecrow of a man, unsure how to take him. He certainly didn't look like an academic let alone a Director of one of the greatest collection in the world.

'Hi. Van Aertsen.' Van Aertsen held his hand out. 'At the moment, we are unable to make…'

The Director ignored the offered hand, 'God man! Can you not do something about this? It's gobbling up my paintings. Priceless works of art that are irreplaceable.'

Appeasing him, Scorel said. 'It is tragic Director and we are trying our upmost to bring an end to this before any more of your invaluable treasures are lost.'

The Director paused and changed his tune. Immediately liking this Amazonian beauty, he flipped his hair, returned a smile and before he could begin flirting, his moment was spoilt by the utterance of the other scientist.

'I believe there is a limit to how long this mass can continue to grow.' Morales stated. 'Its zenith must soon be at maximum point. It should soon slow down, if not stop. At this volume, it cannot last.'

'How long is a piece of string?' the Director questioned him in irritation. 'Before all of my collection, the nation's heritage is extinct and the building is completely...' He stopped and spinning around, he looked at each painting in the room and then the unwelcome 'blob.' He flicked his mane and neighed. 'What are you all doing standing about. Can you not start removing my paintings?'

There was an obvious silence.

He may have looked and behaved like Blackadder's Prince Regent but he did have a point. No one had thought to suggest this. In all the commotion, they had forgotten basic emergency procedures which included the removal of the valuable collection. The gallery staff present could have slapped each other's foreheads.

Immediately with the help of the Fire crew and the Army they began to mobilise and carefully take what paintings they could off the walls. The uselessness and hostilities of earlier were now forgotten as both teams now had something useful to do.

Chuffed with himself, the Director enjoyed the view of the incredibly tall and attractive scientist until his mood was interrupted again by 'Sir? I must now insist you leave this area and evacuate the premises.'

The Director tried staring the Captain down but on spotting the Captain's revolting boil, he subtly began retreating. He also remembered he respected the Queen's soldiers, was as patriotic as the queen's bum and this was a disagreement that he would never dare get into. Trying not to eyeball the boil again, he nodded his head like a puppet. 'Yes. Yes of course.'

Relishing his authority, the Captain had not noticed the Director's repugnance. 'My men here will escort you off the premises for your own safety and believe me sir, we will do everything in our power to protect this country's treasures.'

The Director had to admit his partiality to the Captain's flag-waving words but not his boil. He turned to the scientists and in a sudden surge of rousing, implored, 'Do stop this menace, won't you?'

Scorel, Van Aertsen and Morales all nodded vigorously and in synchronicity and with that the Director galloped out of the room with the other suits led by two soldiers. But not before the Director made his last impression. He somehow tripped on air and fell to his bony knees. Embarrassed before his companions, he got up before they could assist him.

'Someone mend that bloody floor.' He flustered and pointed at a random spot.

He swished his mop of hair back off of his face and was gone. Some tittering was heard in the room.

Rita had taken to directing the Army and Fire Brigade in the removal of the paintings and there was no time for subtleties. She told them 'Just rip 'em off the walls. Don't worry about the plaster or expensive wallpaper, there won't be any walls left soon. As long as they remain in their frames, they'll be fine.'

And so they piled them up in the elevators and lumbered them down the staircase to the waiting military trucks outside the building.

It was an off-the-wall sight witnessing all the men yanking invaluable works of art off the walls. The scene represented a 'free for all.'

While this commotion played out, Rita gazed back at the 'blob' again and again. Drawn to it hypnotically and customarily her musings returned to Eve.

This is ridiculous! It can't be her? How is it possible that this monstrosity is Eve Green? Trying to comprehend it was giving her a migraine.

I couldn't care less anymore. For my own sanity, I ended up avoiding her as much as I possibly could and fobbed her off to management and HR. Who did she think I was? Her Mother? Mother Teresa?

Eve had finally ruined what respect and patience I had. No manager would have given her half as much as I did and now to my better judgement, or lack of it, I feel used and abused. I had even bent the rules to make it easier for her yet she, akin to a mercenary took advantage of my good nature.

The 'blob' farted or was it the Red Queen and Rita cackled. A soldier walking past with a 'Titian' had heard it too and joked, 'I wonder whether it smells?' and Rita cackled some more.

Probably smells of bullshit, she amused herself and returned to her musings. For so long the Red Queen was untouched and it was I who had given her a kind of diplomatic immunity and the repercussions I have to and still do deal with. Me, of all people did not see it until it was too late. All the bickering and adversity she had wrath in the team, fighting with colleagues was a popularity contest to her. She has ripped the team apart, upset a lot of fine hard working and respectable people. She knew only how to insult and deceive, reviled behind backs out of envy because she could not find that well-being herself. God! She was so twisted out of gear!

It got to the point where so very unlike me, I wanted her to get sacked! It would certainly make a lot of people's working lives easier.

She continued to watch the 'blob,' looking for validation or anything that could reveal that it was actually Eve. 'Was there anything left of her in that gunk? Of all the destruction she was wrecking. Was this a continuation of her spitefulness?'

She twchewed; 'What nonsense! What in heaven am I asking? That thing ain't her. It's just a freak of nature. Nothing human whatsoever.'

Rita realised she was haranguing herself for the absurdity of it all and yet she could not escape that part of her sober intellect. That aside from the illogicalness of it all, that it could actually be real. The rational and irrational were butting head to head in her head!

'Ahh, fuck it! It's doing my head in. I need a drink!'

The 'blob' had now reached the centre of the room. Where it would go was anyone's guess. It was at a crossroad with three other exits beckoning.

All the paintings had been removed from the room and more of the military were called in to start removing the art from threatened adjacent rooms.

The scientists were within three feet of it now much to the jumpiness of the Captain. He almost piggy-backed them as they scrutinised the glutinous like mutation and so engrossed where they by the phenomena, they hardly noticed him.

'… the biological process which usually in an animal, physically develops after birth or hatching. It involves an abrupt change in the animal's body structure through cell growth and differentiation. It is commonly accompanied by a change of habitat or behaviour but in this case, it seems the reverse. Her distorted behaviour may have triggered it off.'

'Morales, Are you suggesting…'

'Yes Scorel.' He cut her off. He did not like to be interrupted even though he seemed to think it was acceptable for him to do so. 'Hyper-metamorphosis is a term used in entomology and also in psychology. It refers to a psychological condition affecting reaction to visual stimuli. Also referred to a mammalian, primate condition where there is excessive and indiscriminate reaction to visual stimulus. A system of 'Klüver-Bucy.' His eyes never wavered from the 'blob,' as if he could behold its bowels.

Van Aertsen disagreed. 'I don't think it is Morales.'

'But what about visual agnosia, Aertsen? Scorel interjected. 'The impulse to notice and react to everything within sight incorrectly and cataclysmically. From what her colleague has told us…' she steeped towards Rita. '…this feels like the classic reaction.'

'That system alone is not enough.' Van Aertsen reminded. 'I will not rule it out but we do not know enough about this person despite the details Rita has shared with us.' His hand went out, palm up towards Rita. It looked like he was about to ask her for a dance. She acknowledged this with a coy smile and tried to look like she knew what they were talking about but felt like the ignorant layman. They may well have been talking in Eskimo!

She also noticed they were addressing each other with their surnames. Was this a professional thing or that the cleverest minds found first names beside the point?

Scorel put in, 'I don't think 'Klüver-Bucy' has anything to do with this Morales. Where's the proof of syndrome resulting from bilateral lesions of the anterior temporal lobe?' There's no ischemia, progressive subcortical gliosis or porphyria.'

'Wake up Scorel. Absence of proof is not proof of absence!' Morales stated. 'Can you not see that what we are witnessing is a new kind of phenomena? He blusterously finished.

'Undoubtedly agreed.' Van Aertsen nodded his head agreeably. 'But we cannot know for sure at this stage Morales. Without a psychiatric evaluation and numerous tests which, as you can see my esteemed colleagues, we cannot perform presently. It will be only later, after the event and an autopsy that we can then start.'

The silence that followed meant he was right. At the moment it was all speculation and educated guesses. Yet something triggered it, Van Aertsen pondered. It was growing uncontrollably, if in an inherently chaotic way and assimilating all matter. A new form of evolution was evident here. Possibly human metamorphosis extant. A marked change in form, texture and physical appearance. A bodily dissipation of sorts and no longer human form. The transformation of the physical and a breaking free of the limitations of its body. Had she, it, the female human she once was given birth to something? No! He was convinced that she was being reborn!

Its texture reminded him of that insulating pink foam sealant used by builders and plumbers. He was curious as to what it felt like and leaned forward for a touch and was engulfed.

It happened so suddenly, nobody could help him. Van Aertsen had no chance as it encompassed his hand, arm, upper body and then all of him with such rapidity that it pulled him into its mass in one swift fluid motion.

For one brief moment all faces present in the room seemed to re-enact Edvard Munch's 'The Scream.'

Morales stumbled to the floor on his derrière then quickly scrambling backwards, dragging himself away from the 'blob' like a dog cleaning its behind. Scorel swayed away like a blustered tree and Rita frozen to the spot, muttered 'God in heaven!'

The soldiers who had pounced forward guns phasing, changed their minds and sprang back while the Captain shouted, 'The bloody fool!' Seemingly more annoyed that this had occurred on his watch.

Everyone else quickly retreated with either backs to walls or prone by doorways, fearful but still intrigued like spectators at the Pamplona Bull Run.

Nothing could be done for the Doctor and then what sounded like a satisfied belch, trumpeted from the 'blob.'

The only people in the room now - as they mourned by the only exit - were the Captain, Dr. Scorel and Prof. Morales. Rita stood with the Fire Chief. His crew and some soldiers hung further back all shaking their heads at each other like a pack of consoling 'Churchill Dogs.'

On the Captain's vocal orders, no one was allowed within a barge-pole of the 'blob.'

Almost all of the room was now filled with it and more spilled into the opposite corridor, practically sealing off that section of the gallery.

Apart from the soft crinkling of the mutant mass, a solemn silence hung in the air since the absorption of Dr. Van Aertsen. They could only assume he was dead. There was no way he could still be alive inside that thing. If he wasn't crushed then surely he suffocated in the enveloping gungy flesh.

Scorel said, 'Nothing like this has occurred before.'

'You can say that again!' Rita remarked sardonically.

'No...' Scorel said slightly uncomfortable with the whole lamentable episode.

'I mean in labs under controlled conditions, yes, but never with a human being. This is all new to us. Dangerous.' She added as an afterthought.

'How can you carry on?' Rita deplored. 'Your colleague is dead!'

'Regrettably, yes.' Scorel said sadly, eyes down. 'But we must. The threat continues and more lives could be lost.' She now gazed at Rita earnestly who reluctantly understood the situation with a nod of her head.

Morales did not wait long, 'Tangibly, it does occur in humans yet in puberty, not so markedly and dramatically.' He was almost whispering though, respectful. 'Van Aertsen's demise is unfortunate but important in terms of a major discovery! This fascinating phenomenon is possibly one of a kind and we are the first to witness it.'

'What you said earlier Scorel, its subtle and over a much longer period from childhood to adulthood and barely acknowledged in the nurturing stages, accepted as every day and routine and only remarked upon as growing pains. As a miracle that our early development is, we are observing it here and now at an extreme rate. These kinds of changes occur every day in animals and insects too. This process...' he pointed at it. '... of metamorphosis. We are witnessing for the first time in a human being what is only a matter of time and evolution.'

Scorel was beginning to understand her esteemed colleague but she was the only one.

Morales continued, 'If metamorphosis is understood to comprise the processes of dramatic change whereby a juvenile reaches maturity both sexually and biochemically, then human puberty may be considered a variation of the metamorphic theme. Remember what...' He had forgotten Rita's name. Actually he never paid attention to introductions or first names. Gesturing Rita, he said, 'The lady told us about.....' He had forgotten the guard's too and Rita said 'The Re...' She coughed. 'Eve.' She said too brashly.

'Eve possibly showed signs of a late developer. An underdeveloped woman hence her playground mentality. Cortical immaturity. Possible adolescent growth spurts that had not occurred in the usual manner. Very protracted and not at all uncommon.'

Scorel nodded like a tree in the wind. 'These are definitely parallels to late puberty. Lack of development to sexual maturity and subsequent physiology.'

So she hadn't really grown up. Rita deduced. She had been listening and despite the scientific jargon she was starting to get the gist of it. Her own musings had considered a childish aspect to the Red Queen's behaviour.

'I don't get how Eve could have turned into that though?' Rita asked the obvious.

Morales looked at something behind her and answered. 'Morphogenesis. It is the biological process that causes an organism to develop its shape. The control of cell growth and cellular differentiation. Morphogenetic responses may be induced in organisms by hormones, by environmental chemicals. Substances produced by other organisms or toxic chemicals. Mental stresses leading to mechanical stresses.

Yeah right, got that! Rita nodded perplexed as a penguin meeting a polar bear!

'Let me simplify.' Scorel offered the blank faces. 'Usually when stresses, anxieties and dissatisfaction all build up, it tends to lead to a breakdown. We see it all the time but in this case the reaction is remarkable distinct, obviously. The energy and pressure, will and anger caused a mutation. An external reaction like we have never seen before yet the internal is no different. Like a caterpillar into a butterfly but in reverse.'

There seemed some logic to their explanations, Rita thought. But it was still hard to digest.

Poor girl she rued and realised she still cared for her. Well the person she was once and not this grotesque thing she had become. It felt surreal and askew despite observing the CCTV footage of the human Eve turning into 'blob' Eve. She had carried some kind of mental illness like baggage to the point it became a physical sickness and like an elastic band she stretched herself to snapping point. In her case highly nihilistic too. Pulling and tugging it herself in a form of self-harm.

Sigourney Weaver was talking again, 'The fact that she has consumed innocent lives has only made her unhinged.'

Rita remembered van Aertsen and realised her sympathy for the Red Queen was not justified. The dear departed handsome devil merited her compassion and also the two earlier victims.

'So your hypothesis is Scorel, that there is still a consciousness, a mind prevailing amongst that mass?' Morales sceptically asked.

'It's only a hypothesis but quite possibly, she knows what she has done.'

Yeah! She has murdered people by swallowing them alive. Rita coldly stated to herself. God, it's sick!

Ludolf had been reading a novel about this very building being taken over by Nazi terrorists and some hidden gold when he was interrupted by the Security Head on the phone.

'Ludolf, you got only another hour before we all have to get out of the building. It's becoming too dangerous. I will come by once I know everybody else is out and we can leave together. Make sure you have set all evacuations procedures.'

'Yep! Yep! Will do.' He replied nonchalantly and went back to his book. He was near the end and wanted to finish it and the constant interruptions were not helping.

Occasionally he glanced up at the monitors and noticed more of the rooms filling up with the pink stuff and eventually each CCTV camera turned to static as it too was consumed, the image lost.

The radio chatter was a buzz of static and squawks. Nothing important to him and it meant he had less distractions. As he read his book and ate a Cornish pasty, flakes of crumbs made their home in the pages of his book and his lap.

He had not really given much thought to the crisis. He was expecting it to end at any moment and it would just be another minor incident like a blocked toilet or an electrical black out that occurred every now and then. He was convinced the 'blob' would soon disappear like the odours of bad cooking that sometimes set off the alarms. As regards to the damage, well things were easily replaced and just like the paintings could be restored.

Behind him was the only exit and entrance to the Control Room and on the adjacent wall close to floor level the pastel solferino substance began to spill silently through the vent into the room. What was remarkable about its movement and behaviour was the lack of sound it made. There was none of the familiar crackling and popping that it usually discharged. It was as silent as air and stealth-like. It did not take long before it had converged by the door and begin to grow tall and cover it completely.

Ludolf was so engrossed by his book that he was completely oblivious to what was happening behind him until the 'blob' decided to be heard. It burped with such force that Ludolf jumped in his seat with a scream. Choked on his pasty and splatter-coughed over a monitor.

He turned to see the pink stuff looming towards him like a giant leech or an incarnadine Triffid.

'It's in my room!' he screamed the obvious. His eyes wanted to disbelieve and he began to moan like a distraught child.

The 'blob' had formed what looked like the shape of a head on top and it writhed from side to side like it was mocking him. It towered seven feet in the small Control Room and an orifice began to open in the middle of its mass, pronouncing a sucking sound.

As it approached him closer, Ludolf could only formulate in his mind that this thing wanted to kiss him and how disgusting that was. It looked different to the images he had observed on the screens. In real life, it had a wet sheen to its surface and was much more gelatinous in substance and menacing too.

He couldn't get out of his chair quick enough because of his weight and it wasn't going anywhere trapped up against the console. He started to wheeze like an asthmatic

Whoopee Cushion, his protruding and overfed stomach rising and falling erratically. Clothing sweat soaked, he began to dribble from one corner of his crumb covered mouth. His frightened eyes jumped about looking for a way out and realised he could not move from fear.

The mass started to curve towards him on each side, surrounding him and to all appearances looking like it was leaning in for a hug.

Now a few feet from him the orifice akin to a mouth widened, the sucking contortions hungry-like and he could clearly make out the viscosity of its skin. Its living semi-transparent flesh. It actually looked like a vagina that wanted to kiss him!

A thought struck and it was terrifying. Is this the Red Queen? Was she in there somewhere? That she somehow, innately still existed and was coming for him out of spite, hatred, revenge? He proceeded to wet his pants.

He was now completely surrounded and yet it held back from touching, engulfing, swallowing him. Swaying closer and closer in front of him in a hypnotic teasing dance.

There was a faint odour about it. An oxidant bleach-like smell and he realised it smelt like hair dye.

'Fuck me!' he uttered in disbelief.

And in a metaphorical sense, the 'blob' did.

It was no longer a she! Some would say it had given up human form as soon as she popped. Surely there could be nothing resembling a person in that? Rita wondered.

Inside its impenetrable mass, it must have had a substance; an acid that quickly broke down, melted and assimilated all the foreign substances that it had swallowed up. Furniture, fittings, paintings, people too including poor Dr. van Aertsen, all entirely absorbed with not a single trace of their existence remaining but the memories and nightmares in all of us that had observed and witnessed this unbelievable but tragic event.

'Look!' A fireman pointed and everyone did. The 'blob' had started to turn in on itself, a slow gradual implosion. Forms began to appear in its pinkish translucence. A chair and a bench could be made out. A blender kaleidoscope of multi-layered images surfacing and disappearing in a whirlpool of shifting shapes of putty or magma. Churning and turning over and into itself again and again. Abstract friezes revolved like an ever evolving piece of art of the paintings which themselves had been consumed by it.

Then horror! Did Rita catch a glimpse of Prof. van Aertsen? His head and out-stretched arms?

Fleeting as it was, she dismissed it as folly. In all that twirling and swirling and over-lapping of layers, it would have been easy to make out what you wanted. It would be akin to gazing at clouds long enough.

Looking closely, you could see a Rembrandt, a Vermeer, a large wooden piece of the chest-like Peepshow by van Hoogstraten and a Rubens landscape. All these artworks briefly represented in a fudge-like version until finally a brief glimpse or representation of a woman's face, her face, the Red Queen!

Medusa like and appearing to scream but her silent dilating mouth and discernible features only appeared more frightened and terrified in its agonising contortions. Suddenly my heart went out to her. I remembered the sweet young lady that joined the gallery, my team five years ago. I wanted to forget all the troubles she had caused, all the spiteful games she had played. Those lost traits did occasionally surface some days like a distant memory. Etch-A-Sketch lines reminding me, us, of the woman she once was but the havoc and wreckage she left in her wake, made it difficult to forgive.

Her colleagues and the National Gallery wouldn't forget the woman. Their pink-headed colleague with the temper and egregious fire-branding. And as much as many of us would deny it, we did speak about her. She was right in some aspects but that alone was not her downfall.

The world too would come to know her name as the woman who blew her top and destroyed the planet!

Rita finally uttered something she had wanted to get off her chest for a very long time and she felt so much better for it. 'Selfish bitch!'

Every single vehicle and crew of the City of London Fire Brigade was now on site. Thousands of soldiers of the British Army were mobilised and with the assistance of the Greater London Police, continued to evacuate the habitual public from the seething streets, exorbitant bars, expensive restaurants and outrageous theatre seats. Residents were also pulled from their properties.

Still nothing could be done to stop the rampaging and out of control 'blob!'

The two specialists, Scorel and Morales remained nearby observing and ad-libbing in their own exuberant fascination while sipping hot chocolate like it was bonfire night. Still unable to help avert this plague, their expertise was now about as useful as a fortune cookie.

'It's a menace!' The Director could be heard blathering like a domestic doomsayer. Understandably so, nevertheless the majority of the nation's treasured art collection had been removed but he was still a 'ponce' about it.

Surrounding him was a pool of reporters and cameras and all the People around the world watching on their humongous televisions wondered who was this jerk that kept flipping his floppy hair like a model in a shampoo advert?

All the emergency services could do was to keep moving and pushing the growing number of people back, back, back. If you strained your ears and listened carefully, you could hear the Captain shouting those familiar orders over the din of screaming people and crumbling buildings. It was all he and the Army could do despite him foolishly believing a well-placed missile could put a stop to this monstrosity once and for all.

The Fire Chief continued to have 'critical meetings' with his superiors to no avail. The men unproductive, held hoses and equipment like flaccid penises.

Rita was safely a thousand yards away from the danger zone and just as well as the sight before her and on all the TV news channels around the globe replayed the images of the iconic National Gallery covered in what looked like pink Play-Doh. It seemed the more it consumed the bigger it grew. Feeding and growing, everything was food and there was plenty of it for the Red Queen to greedily gobble up.

Rita soon felt cold and exhausted and proceeded to go home to her bottle of Prosecco.

It would continue to spread. Unstoppable it was. Destroying and consuming the gallery and outside; the West End streets, buildings, infrastructures and all of London. Eventually the country in an all devouring pink goop!

And every single human being whether in their head, humming, whistling or singing aloud would know the 'Armageddon Song.'

'Red and green should never be seen.
She's best avoided the Red Queen.
She swelled and swelled,
Lost her temper and ruined the world!'

Afterword

This story very much feels it has much in common with the 'Terrorvision' album 'How to make friends and influence people.' In my mind, I hear it as the soundtrack to this story. It is also a homage to the golden age of science fiction stories and movies that still thrill me with their ideas to this day.
December 2015

I would like to thank......
The handy Free Dictionary App by Farlex, my time-saving companion Notebook and my 'best present ever' iPod for the continual momentum.
Caroline too and 'It's all good' Lance.
My Geeky Girl Blue for doing all the technical stuff and producing the final package once again.
And a huge thanks to all my compelling colleagues and friends (past & present) for their support and fellowship at the National Gallery. This is for you.